ROY JOHNSON

Roy the Gargoyle

Trafford
PUBLISHING™

Order this book online at www.trafford.com/07-1542
or email orders@trafford.com

Most Trafford titles are also available at major online book retailers.

Note for Librarians: A cataloguing record for this book is available from Library
and Archives Canada at www.collectionscanada.ca/amicus/index-e.html

ISBN: 978-1-4251-3851-6

*We at Trafford believe that it is the responsibility of us all, as both individuals
and corporations, to make choices that are environmentally and socially sound.
You, in turn, are supporting this responsible conduct each time you purchase a
Trafford book, or make use of our publishing services. To find out how you are
helping, please visit www.trafford.com/responsiblepublishing.html*

*Our mission is to efficiently provide the world's finest, most comprehensive
book publishing service, enabling every author to experience success.
To find out how to publish your book, your way, and have it available
worldwide, visit us online at www.trafford.com/10510*

 www.trafford.com

North America & international
toll-free: 1 888 232 4444 (USA & Canada)
phone: 250 383 6864 ♦ fax: 250 383 6804 ♦ email: info@trafford.com

The United Kingdom & Europe
phone: +44 (0)1865 722 113 ♦ local rate: 0845 230 9601
facsimile: +44 (0)1865 722 868 ♦ email: info.uk@trafford.com

10 9 8 7 6 5 4 3 2

Contents

＊

The Moving Shadows on
the Church

It's raining cats and dogs, very cold and wet; a person could see his own breath in the darkness of this dreadful night. Roy stands in the rain, no umbrella, wet as hell, but not one sign of a pant or even cold air leaves his mouth. He watches the kid, a five foot nine, one hundred and fifty pound Caucasian, with short black hair; His shiny mousse filled hair repels the rain. He has tattoos around his neck and wears a long, black trench coat. Walking down Western Avenue, he crosses the street and looks back; He senses eyes following him, but doesn't see Roy.

Every half block, Roy makes his move; damn, he's fast for a guy who has the look and size of a football player. The kid reaches his point, that church over there, the tall, ancient, dark building, with ugly wicked look-ing creatures dangling around it, water gushes from their mouths. Roy's across the street between two buildings, using the newsstand as a cover to help hide his presence. The kid has this mad look on his face; His brown eyes, full of fear and hate, looks up at the rain; he feels something in the air. He shakes his head to the left and right; He knows somebody's watching him, but he's too mad to even care. With brewing anger, the kid reaches for the handle, and enters the front door of the church.

Outside, the drenching patters resound the pavement. Roy's waiting, but he stands still, looking like one of those mimes you see on the Promenade in Santa Monica; You don't see him breathe, but he's breathing, you don't see him move, but he's moving. He looks at the top of the building and notices all the oddly, hideous monstrous appearances of gargoyles, around the corners of the building; A smirk goes over his face; there's something about these statues which amuses him. During his muse, a frown quickly paints his face; He smells it, that smell. The rain, as rivers, flow into his eyes, but he doesn't blink, not once. Roy's got his eyes fixed on the top center of the building, right where the doors go up toward one of the gargoyles, which arches over the entrance.

The weirdness of such events; everyone has faced one of these moments. It is where you feel something in the room or around you, or in the air, but you can't see it, where you get cold chills, but it's not cold, where you feel something dreadful, but nothing is there, and realize that there's something creepy and nasty going on, but you can't place your finger on it. In these situations, most people get to a location or point where they shake it off as nothing, and go about their usual business, or they get to where people are, or to a television, or radio, anything that brings them back to regularity. Smelling something when it is raining so hard and the poor visibility in the pouring rain makes it even more of a horrible situation, that any sane person would escape; but not Roy, he smells it, and he's waiting for it.

Three minutes, there they are, he sees them. They are black shadows, something that very few ever get to see. At most, one is all a person ever sees in the glimpse of a moment, and most people don't ever notice the shadow; But this time, There are a thousand of them. These shadows are unlike other shadows, they move together as one. They are moving fast, all over the top of the building in swarms; the dark glides towards the front door. Roy knows he only has a couple of minutes to take action. His feet, although heavy, are fast as lightning. In just four seconds, he's at the door.

He never looks up or around at the shadows; as he reaches to open the door, the shadows stop as in shock to see his presence. They make no sound; they just look down at him as he enters the church. The door quietly shuts behind Roy, as he looks into the dim lighted chapel with murals; there are candles on the wall and marble everywhere. Roy walks through the foyer into the main chapel, where sits the kid up front. He stops at the back pews and watches the kid. The kid is just sitting, and staring at the crucifix of Jesus. He has no idea that anyone is watching. Two minutes, Roy smirks and walks forward. The weight on his shoes makes a squeaking sound, causing the kid to turn his head a little, as he looks out the corner of his eye, then back to the front, staring at the crucifix.

✳

The Vampires Walk

Roy walks towards the right center aisle to the front of the chapel, his shoes drenching wet, his coat's soaked from top to bottom; he never once takes the time to wipe his wet face. As he walks toward the front, to sit one pew behind, on the right side of the kid, who sits on the front pew, the kid shakes his head in a negative way, while continuing to stare at the crucifix. "What's up?" says Roy, throwing his head back in an upward motion. "I ain't trying to hear you bro." replies the kid. He bellows, "Oh, my fault dog." Roy begins again, "Is this your church?" The kid is looking over his right shoulder, down behind him, out the corner of his angry eyes, peering at Roy's shoes, in a wispy manner, "You the janitor or something?" "Naw man." exclaims Roy.

He notices the kid looking down at his shoes. "Oh, my shoes; you're looking at my shoes." With anxiousness, Roy explains, "These ain't work boots, I know they look like it, but I've worn these down a little bit; Actually, I had them specially made, and they just wore out on me; These are my combat boots." Roy points over the pew at the kids shoes. "And you got on those big old black gothic looking stackers, those look a lot like the ones I've got on now!" The kid is still looking forward at the crucifix with that same mad look on his face.

Roy starts to speak and is interrupted, "I didn't come here for talk." "Word, word." Roy gestures in a low tone, while nodding yes. "I've got some business to take care of." the kid says in a cynical tone. "See, I came here for the same reason you did, I have some business to take care of too." The kid replies in a smart aleck way, "How do you figure?" "You don't even know me bro, I didn't come here for prayer or for any forgiveness, I don't believe in this religion." Roy expresses with enthusiasm, "See, I told you we came here for the same reason, I don't believe in religion either." The kid, ticked off, speaks, "You don't know what the fuck I'm here for!"

Roy gives a stern look at the back side of the kids face and begins, "You think I can't see, I get it, you've got all that black on and shit, fucking piercing everywhere, a long assed black trench coat and combat boots with fricken chains everywhere straight up in the middle of church on a cold assed rainy Monday night, and you ain't religious? Damn, a blind man could see that some shit's about ready to go down, dog!" Roy struggles with showing emotion, since his kind doesn't really care to exercise emotion, but he uses it to get his point across to the kid. The kid has a smirk on his face, while thinking to himself that this Negro is amusing and funny, and really could see what was going on in his head.

"You ain't a pig." says the kid, still looking at the crucifix. "Hell naw, I'd rob a liquor store, go down to the local coffee shop where the little oinks hang out and smoke a blunt right in front of their face, while eating a doughnut, cause I got the damn munchies." Roy continues ranting, "Outcast hell, I know all about being an outcast, fuck em, fuck em all! I don't have no beliefs, I don't believe in church, I sure the hell don't believe in these fake assed priest and preachers up in this place, from politics to lunatics from aliens to ghost, hell, it's all a game, and if you're caught up in it, shit, you're gonna get played!"

In amazement of what Roy's saying, the kid with a frown, speaks out in rebuttal, "Everybody believes in something, even atheist believe in something. They claim to not believe in anything, but the very belief that they don't believe in anything is a belief!" Roy interrupts "I don't believe in atheist." "How can you not believe in atheist, they exist, they are there, they are real people." Roy's smiling, he's being sarcastic. He begins again, just to see what the kid would say to him, "Just because I see them, don't mean I have to believe them." The kid gets frustrated with Roy's logic and makes a comparison. "Do you believe that there is air?" "Of course I believe that there is air." Roy, appearing wild eyed with disgust. "Can you see air?" Looking curious, Roy is sure he can see air, but he doesn't want the kid to think he's crazy, so he replies, "No, I can't see air." The kid speaks up, "So you believe in things you don't see, and don't believe in things you do see."

"Look, uh, what's your name?" "John." "I'm Roy." He speaks in haste, "Look John, I can't see ghost, you know why I can't see ghost, because they don't exist! I don't believe in ghost, I don't believe in aliens, devils, angels, witches, goblins, elves or fucking Santa Clause, okay?"

John replies, "Hey, I'm not saying that I believe all those things either, but there's a difference in believing in what people believe in and believing in the actual people that believe in those things themselves. There are some things that are real and some things that are not. Take for instance, the people who run this church, I don't believe in their faith or their God, but I have respect and know that they are real people who have beliefs."

Roy replies to John, "Hey, don't tell me that you don't have beliefs in this religious malarkey, cause I know you're probably sitting right here thinking of a way to conjure up some kind of demon or something to help you take care of your fucking business; Well that's just bull shit, cause it ain't real; The only thing that's real is the crazy mother fuckers that believe in this crap!" John becomes hostile and replies, "You just fucking watch your mouth bro, because demons are real!" Roy hits John's nerve point blank; he can see it in his eyes, the hate, and the anger. John is one second from pulling his 22 automatic from under his trench coat and blowing Roy's head off.

John has this wild look in his eyes, not one blink, just a long hard ass stare of pure hate. Roy, being aware of the tense moment, while looking right at John, who's head is turned back fully, he starts to say something, when John yells out in anger, "You mean to tell me that you don't fucking believe in nothing, No demons, witches, or vampires?" Roy's eyes gets big, and in a surprising tone, "Vampires, you didn't say nothing about no damn vampires!" John doesn't know how to respond and is astonished. "You've got to be fucking kidding me man! You believe in

10

vampires, but you don't believe in demons or ghost? Shit, you've lost it bro, you've fucking lost your mind!"

The wild look leaves John's eyes as he laughs inside, while he turns his head back around, facing the crucifix, nodding his head, that someone is more twisted in their mind then he could ever be. It gets silent for a half of minute, when Roy starts, "Vampires, shit, you don't have to tell me about vampires, that's real!" John starts to let out these short silent chuckles.

"Vampires are real man, I'm serious." John shakes his head in ridicule of Roy's twisted humor of believing in nothing, but believing in vampires. John answers, "How can you possibly justify your belief in something that you've never seen and then condemn people who do the same, huh?"

Roy exclaims, "What the hell are you talking about man? See-see you don't understand. Vampires aren't like the vampires you read in books, hear on the radio, see on television or watch at the movies; Naw man, vampires are real!" "How do you figure?" John waits for Roy to explain it. "Vampires are people just like you and me everyday, in everyday life. They eat, sleep, have sex, smoke cigarettes, hell, you even see them in the daytime. You've just got to have eyes to see them, that's all." John replies, "Vampires huh?" Roy wants to prove his point, "The average vampire doesn't have fangs, sleep in coffins, or turn into bats, or mice, or any kind of rodent; No, they are everyday people just like you and me. John asking, "So how do you know what they look like?"

Roy responds, "It's not just what they look like, but what they do, and how they act. Most vampires are extremely athletic, they have incredible strength, but the freaky part is that they don't have to work out to get these nice bodies. Many of them are contortionist, it's very hard to break their bones, and if they do, they usually heal in a very short time frame, like a month or so. They can be any ethnicity. Over seventy five percent of them are extremely attractive, and they are very seductive, and addicted to sex; they have a certain charm about them."

Roy continues, "Vampires are sensitive to light, especially the sun. Don't be fooled though, they can go out in the day light. With sunscreen, they can be out in the sun, but they do tend to have fair skin and can burn easily. The one's that are closer to death usually comes down with some sort of skin cancer; the extreme cases are melanoma, which is known to kill them off in just a few weeks or months. Other than that, they live long lives. Some of the stronger vampires fake their identity, because of their age. Their aging is delayed, as the usual vampire lives to be well over a hundred." By this time, Roy really has Johns attention, as John who has turned his body all the way around, with his knees against the back of the pew where he sits, his boots are hanging off the end of the seat, his trench coat is ruffled from his twisted torso, he's into what Roy is saying.

Roy looks at John who's spellbound; It's time for the know all catcher all response. He leans closer to John's face and makes his finale. "Above all, there are two most important things a person must know about vampires. One; His eating habits." John replies, "Is that right?"

Roy speaks calmly, "Yeah, that's right. You have to know how and what a vampire eats. A real vampire doesn't suck the blood from the veins of his victim, but he could if he wanted to. They feast off blood, but it doesn't have to be humans. Vampires just love blood, any kind of blood; however, their other prized appetite for drinking is wine, especially red wine. Red wine, because there are a lot of similarities between drinking red wine and drinking blood. They love wine, red wine. Besides wine and blood, their favorite food is steak, rare or medium rare. A vampire loves to eat red meat, the more rare the food the stronger the vampire. There's one thing you must know too; when they're eating, they get wild afterwards, or after they have feasted on such blood. It's like they get drunk off it. They love to party hardy. The nightclubs are their feeding ground, especially the ones that sell steak and wine, and let's not forget about all the sex that go on with the nightclub life. The second and most important of them all is the walk. Now, this is the shit, which separates the men from the boys! The vampires walk is graceful. They almost walk on their toes at times. They look like stallions or professional Arabian dancing or walking horses. There's nothing more attractive but yet wicked as a vampires walk. Their legs are exotic. They love to dance, but when they walk, it underlines the expression *catwalk,* cause these mother fuckers can prance their asses off. Their spring is in their step, you've got to watch that shit!" "Vampires?" replies John, in disbelief. Roy gets up, walks around the right side saying, "John, I'm going to tell you a story of how I whipped Dracula's ass." "Dracula, the Dracula?" John hisses. Roy sits next to John and gives him a serious look. "The one and only Count Dracula, the same one you've read about in books, I mean the stories change but the gist of it is still the same." John speaks in a sarcastic way, "You beat Dracula?" "Yeah, I beat his ass, that one you and everybody else calls Dracula. Dracula, he had that same walk, those same moves. I don't think there could have been a slicker more graceful, heartless, intelligent person who could have coined such talent as in a walk. This shits magical!"

The Mysterious Light

Roy can almost taste the blood, the same blood that he tasted that night which changed his life. He looks at John with earnestness, and begins. "I was stationed in Egypt." John growls, "So you were in the military and those are your actual combat boots." "Hear me out now; General Steve C. Marshall of the 82nd Airborne division gave me orders to deploy in Giza Egypt, a tourist area where laid a Sphinx and a Pyramid. I have two units, that's a hundred and fifty strong, and I'm their commanding officer."

Roy sits right side of Major Thomas M. Scarborough, Colonel Reginald E. Wade and Lieutenant Colonel Bradley N. McDouglas. In walks Brigadier General Steve C. Marshall. "Gentlemen, As usual, you know why you're here." General Marshall slaps his pointer on the face of the Sphinx. "We have terrorist attacks at this area. Scarborough, do what you do; I want you to have Johnson on the ground by O nine hundred. Johnson, scramble like a squirrel hunting a nut, I know I can depend on you. Once the both of you have set up camp, Wade and myself will join you with reinforcements." Major Scarborough interrupts,

"Reinforcements?" General Marshall, in a stern raspy voice, "Major, don't question me boy, now get your asses out their and do it."

A nine year experienced soldier, who specializes in close quarter combat and covert exercises, All Americans, Captain Roy E. Johnson and his company of the United States Army 82nd Airborne, subdivision elite group, Panther, Dragon, and Green Beret deploys at 0600 and lands at 0900, and executes operation KEEP OUT. Roy in a gushy tone, "Let's get this inventory over with." First Sergeant Matthew D. Lawson in a nervous voice reads the list. "Two MI Abrams Tanks, four M2 Bradley Fighting vehicles." Roy reads along and clamors, "What the hell is this crap?" Lawson, shocked, stops reading, "Sir?" "What kind of ammunition is this, silver impact bullets with semisolid material. What the hell is that supposed to mean, semisolid material? Sergeant, I want you to do your research and find out what that is." Lawson responds, "I already have sir." "You have, well what is it?" "Gel sir." Roy replies in a mordant way, "Gel? What kind of gel are we talking here; Is it jello, hair gel, K.Y. Jelly?" Lawson, surprised, answers, "No sir, it's antifreeze." "Antifreeze?"

Roy screeches. "What kind of crap is this, who ordered and what the heck is this stuff for?" "It was a direct order from Central Command." Roy snatches the invoice out of Lawson's hands, and hurries to the last page and sights the signature, Brigadier General Steve C. Marshall. Roy gasps, looks up, shakes his head and looks at Lawson, "Keep this to yourself; I don't want my men to know about it; that's an order." "Sir, yes sir." "Dismissed." Lawson salutes with grace, pivots and walks out.

Roy starts to take his seat, when in, barges Major Scarborough. "Major Sir." Roy salutes. "At ease Captain." "I am to rendezvous with General Marshall at O nine hundred at COM Center. I know I'm in good hands; Carry on with the mission and await our return tomorrow at O nine hundred." Scarborough starts out the door, Roy intervenes, "Sir." "Yes Captain?" "Permission to speak freely sir." "Permission granted." "It's been a month and no action, my boys are getting edgy, If we don't get some kind of break or something, they're going to fucking eat that Sphinx out there for dinner. What's our budget? We need some beer, women, hell, a sheep will do, you know what I mean?"

Scarborough rebukes quickly, "COM'S not going to send you guys anything, and especially not liquor." He turns and starts out the door.

Roy mean-mugs the back of his head, "So what the hell you want me to do?" Half way out the door, he stops in his step, hesitates, slants his head and says, "It's Saturday, throw em a party." He walks out briskly. Roy knows exactly what he means; it's party time for the boys tonight.

Two transport vehicles return with the screech of hydraulic breaks and stops in the middle of camp, where out jumps Second Lieutenant Tyler D. Smith and twenty troopers hauling cases of beer and food. From the second transport vehicle bounces driver Private Vince L. Miles and passenger Specialist Henry M. Smallback. Miles races to the back of the transport yelling, "Look what daddy brought home for junior!" There are fifty one nurses who were part of a previous operation with the 101st division. There's a holy roar from the whole camp. It's time for the fellas to get busy. This is the usual time that Roy and his fellow officer buddy First Lieutenant Ben U. Wynn let their hair down and play checkers while shooting the breeze. Wearing a green beret, Smallback stands and watches from his post as usual. He really loves the tower, where he's known to snipe a fly off a can from twenty five yards.

"Ben, you win!" Roy smiles. "That's right my home-bee." taunts Ben in a long-winded manner. Roy corrects Ben, That's "Homie." "So, how long have we've been playing checkers Roy?" "Since way back in high school dog." Roy scratches his head. Ben boasts, "Damn, That's a long time, and to think that after all that time of whipping your ass in checkers, you'd learn to beat me by now." "Oh yeah, speaking of asses being whipped, I saw the original inventory." Roy looks surprised. "Oh don't worry, you know me, I've got my buttons in tact, those lips are sealed, But dig this, where do you think that old fart gets the funding to supply a unit of this size with silver? That's a whole lot of Benjamin's and Grants. I knew you could pull strings with the General, but silver bullets, hell that beats them all. What in Gods name are we defending here anyway, a few artifacts, waiting for the General and his special ass sniffers to move these whatever you call it into a safer place? So, here we are, baby sitting and keeping Charlie's hand out of the cookie jar. And where the heck is he, we haven't seen Charlie in months around here. You know what that means Roy?" Roy mummers, "What?" "It means, no action gives me reaction!" Ben slings his right hand into the air.

Ben and Roy's best friends from high school, who just happen to end up in the same unit. Not too many officers can get away with bad mouthing, except Ben. Ben's the kind of person who never bites his tongue, a blatant kind of guy, but he's one of the most respected officers in the infantry, a real All American hero, with one hell of a way of making things plane and out in the open. Besides, he's honest and backs up everything he says with muscle and wits. Roy always listens to Ben; it's always helped him to stay grounded and true to what is actually going on around him, especially during heated moments in combat.

Smallback stands over the table, "Sir, you'd better take a look at this." The smile goes off both Ben and Roy's faces; they know something's up. Roy and Ben climb the tower, were awaits Smallback with binoculars. In a steadiness, he points and hands the binoculars to Ben. "Yeah, I see it, it's a flash. It could be someone playing with a flashlight or something." Ben hands them to Roy, and asks, "You see it?" "Yeah, I see it, that's an awful small flash. I don't think its artillery. Hell, from this distance we'd hear it."

Roy looks at Smallback, "What's the range?" Small back acutely replies, "One mile. It's a souvenir shop." Ben, in relief, "Is that all, oh heck; Captain, let's go souvenir shopping, we can tag a couple of our good guys just in case." Roy gives Ben the look of approval. Ben commands Smallback, "Carry on."

Private Vince L. Miles is as careless and as wild as they come when it comes to a private, but one thing stands in his favor, he's one hell of a mechanic and driver. Miles plays doctor with one of the nurses. Smallback yanks up the Canvas, "Let's go." Miles breathes hard while sweating, "Not now!" He looks back at Smallback who stands firm, serious faced. Miles turns back and kisses the nurse, "Got to go baby." He scraps for his gear and dashes out. Roy commands, "I'm leaving you in charge Second Lieutenant Smith, if we haven't returned in one hour, you know what to do." "Sir, yes sir." exclaims Smith.

The Flaming Sword

The dust flies as the jeep slides to a stop. Out jumps Smallback, and scopes around all parameters of the small squared souvenir shop made of stone and salt. "It's clear." Miles remains in the jeep, he's anxious to get back to camp. Ben and Roy walk in. Behind the glass case counter, wearing a white robe and turban stands an elderly Egyptian with grey and white wavy hair and long beard.

Ben, gazing around as he walks towards the counter, "You have a little bit of everything in here." "Ah yes, we sell many things you like." smiles the Egyptian. Ben notices the merchants' license on the wall. "Your English is pretty good, how long have you've had a business here?" "Ah, many years, since before my grandfather. Many Americans buy souvenir here long time." Roy, glancing at the ceiling, notices the pentagram and Greek writing. There's a picture of a sword engraved beside the inscription. "So, this building's made out of salt?" "Yes, yes" nods the Egyptian.

Roy looks on a wooden shelf at small figurines of the Sphinx. "Two American dollars." laughs Roy. "Hey, Roy, look at these daggers over here." exuberates Ben, who stands at the counter. He knows Roy likes to collect daggers. He takes two long steps towards the counter and speaks with enthusiasm. "Yeah, that's what I'm talking about." Roy eyes sparkle, "Hey, let me see that dagger right there, the one with the face of the lion with the emerald eyes." The Egyptian reaches under the glass counter and hands the dagger to him, "You like?" "Hell yeah." he remarks in an upbeat tone.

As Roy slowly pulls the sheath of the dagger, he brings it closer to his face to get a good look at the design and quality of the blade. He refocuses his eyes, when suddenly; he sees a glimmer just behind the merchant. Something catches his eyes. Roy has a stare; he sets the dagger down as it clanks onto the glass. "Let me see that!" Roy pants, he just fell in love with a silver and gold colored sheath, which houses a long handle, which looks like new brass. The Egyptian turns and points at a bamboo sword, "You like this one?" "No, not that one, that one there." points Roy. "Here?" "No; that one right there, right there in front of your face, the one with the big shiny handle."

The merchant points at another sword, "This one?" "No, that one right there in the corner, standing straight up on that stand, under that blanket." The merchant looks at the sword and turns, "Oh, that one is not for sale." Ben interrupts, "What the hell you mean not for sale, anything in here can be bought, so what makes that sword so special that you won't sell it?" "No, I just cannot sell it, it's not for sale." "How much do you think its worth?" "You don't understand; I can't sell you this sword." "I'll buy it off of you for a couple hundred bucks." "Damn are you crazy Roy, It's not worth a hundred. Most of this stuff in here's junk, it's been here for ages." Bens frantic.

Roy gives a heads up, "I'll pay you three hundred." "No, not for sale." Ben injects, "Are you kidding me? Let's go, we've got to get back anyway." "Wait, hold on Ben." Roy asks, "What's the big deal about this sword?" The merchant glances up at the ceiling. Roy's eyes follow and look up at the ceiling. "Is it some sort of religion, having to do with that up there?" Roy hints upward with his head. "Yes, something like that." answers the Egyptian in a shaky voice. Roy frowns with a smirk of disbelief.

The Egyptian explains that the sword has been in that building since he could ever remember and had never left the building, ever. "Well, how the hell did it get here, somebody had to make it, somebody had to bring it here." As Roy speaks, the Egyptian sees a white flash go across the front entrance. Fear is in his eyes. The Egyptian trembles, "What did you say?" "I want that sword man." exclaims Roy. The Egyptian still looks at the door, then glances at Roy. Again, a flash of a figure races across.

The hands of the Egyptian shake as he places the dagger under the case. His eyes continue to look up, "How much you want to buy for?" Roy looks as the Egyptians hands shake. "Look, I'm not going to hit you or anything, just give me a price, and I will be on my merry way. How about five hundred?" The Egyptian speaks in a desperate stern voice, "Twenty five hundred American dollars." Ben yells, "Are you kidding me Ala-ba-ba? I don't know what side of the world you grew up on, but from where I come from, that's called a crock of shit! Roy, let's get the hell out of here before I break somebody's jaw." Roy holds his hands up, "Wait, wait." Roy gasps, holds his breath, stares at the sword, pauses, bites his bottom lip, and lets out a long breath, "Okay."

Ben shakes his finger while pointing at the sword, "Twenty five fucking dollars, Johnson have you lost your damn mind. That's two thousand and five hundred smacks! Hell, I'll make you a sword for that price, custom design it, place an authentic signature on it and everything!" Roy knows Ben is peeved when he calls him by his last name. "Well I'm not going to hang around for this, are you coming or what?" "Naw, go ahead." "Well how in the hell are you going to get back? "I'll walk." Roy excites. "You're serious, you're really, really serious about this. I'm out of here." Ben furious, places his cap on his head, walks toward the door, stops and turns, "Well, I can't leave you alone sir!" Ben burst sarcastically. Roy commands, "Henry will accompany me."

Ben marches out, "Let's go private." Miles scrambles as he pulls his feet down from the steering wheel, straightens his helmet from off his face, and starts the engine. Miles enquires, "The captain sir?" "He's walking, let's go!" Miles punches it. Dust flies as the wheels spin off. Henry veers into the doorway; he knows what's up, the captains on a shopping spree and just fell out with Ben again. Henry hears a swish and turns to see the dust, which remains from the jeep pulling off. His eyes focus through the lifting dust. He holds his breath, fingers the trigger, and sights his M4's night vision; something's there, but the infrared doesn't pick up an image.

20

The Egyptian hurries the dark blanket around the sword and throws it on the counter. Roy squints his eyes, hardens his brow and wonders why the Egyptian's acting weird. "Be careful with that. That's a twenty five hundred dollar piece you're throwing." Roy slowly counts his money. Sweat pours from the Egyptians face. Roy sees that he's nervous. Concerned, he speaks, "You alright?" "Yes yes, I'm okay, it's a little hot tonight, huh?" Maybe you can have air installed with this money you made tonight." The Egyptian nods and hurries the money into the register without counting it. Roy rubs his chin, and waits for the Egyptian to hand him the sword. Frustrated, Roy lifts the warm blanket, which wraps the sword. He pivots and snarls, "Take care of yourself." The Egyptian rushes behind him. "You have a good night now." He walks briskly, and almost steps on the back of Roys' heels.

Roy notices the swords heavy. He smiles, "Just like I like-em, nice and strong." Roy steps out the door. "Thank you, good day." mutters the Egyptian. The door shuts, and the latches lock. Roy peeks at the sword. He doesn't want to get his fingerprints on the handle. He gazes at it and notices ancient writing on the sheath.

*

Dracula Strikes

The sword is tied with short leather sandal string on the bottom and a long twenty four karat gold lasso with clasps wrapped around the top. Roy unwinds and connects it around his waist; His eyes look right and left. Henry's not in sight. "Snap." The right holster unbuttons, laser points and is ready for action. The night air is cool as the wind hisses behind his ears; the sand dust smacks his skin.

In short paces, he advances with caution. Any sign of movement is sure to meet certain death. "Bam!" Roy flies into the air, landing on his side. Still holding his M-9 pistol, he quickly goes into a one-knee squat. He's shaken up, but not hurt. He sights all around, gets up, holds his breath and listens. The wind blows, it's hard to hear.

"Pow!" one shot. He knows something just passes him, but he didn't hit it. He breathes in, holds his air and waits. His blood boils with anticipation. He yells, "Hee-yah!" drop kicks and is knocked down on his back, and flips backwards onto his feet and cry's out, "Come on!" A flash of lightning hits. "Pow!" the gun fires, and is knocked away, while Roy's right wrist slices open by sharp wings; Blood squirts up his forearm, as his voice squeals, "Aaah!" He goes for his Berretta in his left holster, and is kicked down onto his back. In shock, Roy attempts to get up.

The creature jumps into the air and lands on its feet over Roy's legs. "Slash!" his right cheek gashes open. "Wham!" his mouth spews blood. The creature mounts him and goes for the sheath. He immediately pulls the sword and plunges the end of the brazen edge into the creatures' chest. Blood sprays onto Roys' face and arms. The creature lets out a shrill so loud, that it burst one of Roy's eardrums. Injured, it staggers back.

Roy screams in agony and lets go of the sword, his hands blister from burns. He smells his own skin cooking. He swallows blood and spits out. He uses the back of his hand to wipe his eyes. Gasping for air, his mouth hangs open, and pours out blood and drool. Feeling faint, he focuses his eyes towards the creature.

Standing seven feet tall, with wings, which span twelve foot each, is a long white haired, beautiful, bright crystal blue eyed, snow-white complexioned woman. She's wearing a long, heavy, white luminescent robe. Roy's shocked and marvels at such beauty; the glow emitting from the creature causes Roy to squint his eyes. From her chest, bleeds a silver metallic liquid. She looks down at her wound, then looks up, raises both hands and staggers towards Roy. He sits in an upright position, looks down, and uses both burned hands to grab the sword. He painfully raises the sword, and points it at her. Her eyes look surprised. She squats, spreads her wings, looks straight up, and, "boom!" a flash of lightning, bolts.

Roy blinks his eyes from the painful flash, and opens them; she's gone. Suddenly, "Yowl!" screams Roy. The sword is on fire and there's fire all around his arms, causing his sleeves to burn into his skin. He moans in pain, as tears flow from his eyes. Panting heavily, he looks around and sees a spiral of bluish black fire encircling him. His heart jumps as he lets out a loud gust, and drops the engulfed sword.

Roy's head is shaking; there's a long deep stare of disbelief in his eyes. "Hhhh, Hhhh, Hhhh." Not able to catch his breath, his lips frown in fatigue. Tears stream out. "Momma, Momma, Momma." mourns Roy. *Shell shock's a bitch.* Being weak, his eyes close as he stoops over. A tingling rings his ear and begins to get louder. Reality settles in as Roy opens his eyes and hears gunfire and explosions in the distance. Snapping out of it, he focuses his eyes towards camp. There's an attack on the base.

He looks around himself and finds part of his t-shirt torn off. He uses his boots to hold down the corner of the t-shirt and rips it down the middle. His hands are swollen, blistering black and bloody. Roy painfully uses his left hand to wrap the t-shirt around his right hand, and his right hand wraps his left. The sheath is still tied to Roy's waist. Looking at the sword, Roy scoots down, and gets the sheath under the end of the sword. He slides backwards as the sheath begins to cover the sword. He covers it and spots the dark blanket, and wraps it around the sheath and sword. He struggles to stand, but does, and manages to stand up and stagger east towards the camp.

"There's more of them." exhausts First Sergeant Matthew D. Lawson. "Get on the link and notify the Major again." "Yes sir." shouts Lawson as he pivots and climbs down the tower. On ground zero, front line, Second Lieutenant Tyler D. Smith sites his binoculars and radios Ben. "Sir, there's another pack." "How many?" "Twice as many, maybe a hundred or so." "Take-em out." orders Ben.

Smith and his squad leaders along with seventy ground troopers are equipped with the most advanced weaponry United States money can buy. There's seven Abrams M1 Battle Tanks, seven PZH 2000 Howitzers Tanks, four MIM-104 Patriot Missiles and various rocket launchers and anti-armor artillery. In First Lieutenant Ben U. Wynn's platoon awaits Special Air Operations Troop the Golden Dragons, flying ten AH-64 Apaches, the Golden Knights flying seven UH-60 Black Hawks, and six AH-64 Apache Longbow helicopters.

The East side of the bases front line is under attack. A hundred and six large sandy-reddish to shades of grayish timber wolves, weighing a hundred and seventy-five to two hundred pounds with yellowish-brown eyes approach. Drool and foam spouts from their razor sharp fangs, as they charge at seventy miles per hour. "Damn they're moving fast." excites Smith. The growls are heard, as packs of wolves close in at three hundred yards. "Take-em down." commands Smith. "Boom, Ka-tat-tat-tat." The cracking sound and white glow of firepower flies into the night, slaughtering a wild pack of ambush hungry canines.

On the north side of the camp with forty heavily armed ready troopers, stands Master Sergeant John B. Carter. He radios the tower, "Sir, I have activity a hundred degrees north, at a hundred and seventy five yards." "What's your count?" enquires Ben. "Holy shit! Sir, you'd better take a look." Ben steps over to the north side of the tower. His jaw flutters as he speaks with nervousness, "Take-em out, take-em out." Ben orders his air units, "Mow time." "Yes sir." Sergeant First Class Tim G. Kennedy heads ten Apaches into the air. "Yes sir." responds Staff Sergeant John M. Givens who leads seven Black Hawks. "Yes sir." responds third unit Sergeant Keven L. Pollack, as he heads six Apache Longbows. Three units dispatch into combat, Kennedy's northbound, Givens southbound, and Pollack's team's eastbound. The Golden Dragons and Knights are in action.

The Golden Dragons approach to what seemed an endless number of wolves. Sergeant First Class Tim G. Kennedy reports to the tower "Sir, there's several thousands of them." "Take care of business." Ben directs. "Yes sir." Kennedy acknowledges while commanding his unit, "Cut-em down." Fire spews out the AH-64 Apaches, but there's too many, as the wolves move fast.

The Golden Knights maneuver behind to take upon the oncoming wolves. "Let-em rip." commands Staff Sergeant John M. Givens. The Black Hawks launch their fury, but a few hundred has gotten past front line and has entered the camp. Coming from the east to the camps center is Pollack's team. They are able to stop the first wave of wolves, but more are invading rapidly.

Ben dispatches four battle tanks to the center of the camp to help the few ground troopers. There are six snipers, two in the north tower and four on the ground, holding flank behind sandbanks. These specialists are able to down fifty seven wolves in under twelve seconds. Less than a half of mile, east of the camp, again there's a pack of wolves, but this time, they're larger wolves. "Sir, it's hot." "Fire!" commands Second Lieutenant Tyler D. Smith. Ben turns towards the east side, under amazement, and speaks out, "What the hell?"

Standing seven foot tall, at three hundred and eighty pounds, they run faster than the timber wolves. These are the purebreds, the gruesome, the phantoms of myth; they're werewolves. A man wearing military attire rides on the largest werewolf in the midst of the pack. He approaches the east side. This time, the number is so vast that all, which is seen, is a great sea of glowing eyes.

It's a one on one battle, man against beast. "Fire!" calls Smith. The tanks and missile launchers unload their battle, killing several wolves, but it's not enough. "Aaah." cry some troopers whose bones are heard ripping under the growls of mad dogs. Sergeant Keven L. Pollack heads his unit in to aid, but it's hard to hit the wolves without hitting their own men. The ranks are broken, the camp is under attack.

Gunfire is crossing in all directions, causing soldiers to hit some of their own. "Get him off, get him off!" screams a soldier. "Bang, bang!" the sound of thunder downs the wolf. "No!" screams a trooper as his head rips off. "Ka-pow!" the wolf drops. The werewolves stand from their fours onto their hind legs. Like a bear, they slash soldiers into pieces while others fend off some attacks, the bullets are effective against them, but the ability to out maneuver their speed is hard.

Dressed in a black beret, desert camouflage, with dark brown combat boots, Dracula strikes. Off the back of a werewolf jumps the fend of terror as he rips his way past the soldiers at flashing speed, he heads for the entrance of the Sphinx. There's four snipers behind sand bags, two on the left and two on the right. "Bang, bang, bang!" bullets fly at him, as he breaks their necks, the werewolves slash the others on the right. Dracula commands, as ten massive werewolves' tare at the large door of stone. Growls are heard, while bullets plunge into the crowd of mad fangs, dropping two to the ground. The hinges give, and the large cracking sound causes a shift in the doors weight. Dust emits, making visibility impossible to see the wolves.

Hundreds of timber wolves hasten to the entrance, countering any soldiers and tanks. The tanks are able to continue toward the entrance, but its too late, Dracula's inside. The explosions of missiles resound, as ten tanks line up and hurl fire into the midst of packs. Five minutes into action, and all that's seen is gunfire into the dust.

Lining up behind the tanks, awaits Ben and Second Lieutenant Tyler D. Smith, with sixty one ground troopers. "I don't hear the growls." Smith speaks in a nervous tone. "Hold your fire." commands Ben. "Yes sir." grunts Master Sergeant John B. Carter as he turns towards his men yelling, "Hold-em." The guns silence, as the dust begins to lift. There are mounds of slaughtered wolves everywhere. Ben looks at Lawson who holds advanced heat sensing binoculars, "What do you have?" inquires Ben. "I have two wolves and one man standing westward at point zero sir."

A roar is heard as a werewolf approaches out the entrance, "Rat-tat-tat-tat!" The werewolf howls in pain as it drops to the ground. Ben gestures for a hold of fire. Carter clinches his fist, raises his right arm and speaks, "Hold-em."

Ben looks towards Lawson with anticipation. Lawson responds, "I have one wolf and one man at point zero sir. The wolf's moving towards exit at fifty five meters, fifty four meters, fifty three meters." "Pow-pow-pow!" down drops the wolf, oozing blood from its mouth. Lawson looks through the heat sensing binoculars, "Sir, I have one man unarmed, advancing westward. Wait, he's moving a box." Dracula tares through the two-foot thick lead box, revealing the top and its contents. Lawson's heart flutters, as his eyes get big, "Sir, it reads gamma blue!" "Shit, it could be a nuke." excites Second Lieutenant Tyler D. Smith. Ben radios Master Sergeant John B. Carter. "What's on the speaker?" "Our tanks show gamma off the charts sir." "Jesus, that's over five thousand Kelvin." Smith expels in shock. Ben commands all units to cease-fire. The soldiers drop their firearms in a resting position. Ben hardens his brow, "Lawson get me a fix." "Sir, there are no wires, there are no breaks." The target is turning the box, and has removed the top." Ben gives Smith the look, "Strap up." "Yes sir." calmly replies Smith.

Smith is number one sniper. He mounts the center MI Abrams Tank, lays stomach down, and sites his fifty-caliber sniper rifle at fifty three meters from the Sphinx's entrance. Ben's confident that Smith can down the target. Ben turns his head towards Lawson, "Sir, the target is facing exit and is slowly pacing eastward, carrying the box frontal; the box appears heavy sir. Target is spotted at fifty six meters, fifty five meters, fifty four meters, fifty three meters."

Dracula stands in the Sphinx's entrance holding a large black lead box weighing over two thousand pounds. Smith sites Dracula's head and awaits his orders from Ben. Ben looks to Lawson, "Do we know if it is stable or not?" "Sir, it is stable, but I don't know if it becomes unstable at impact of the human target." Ben looks serious, "Get me the horn, let's see what the freak wants." Ben speaks through a loud horn. "Lay down the box and take two steps back." Ben awaits a response. Dracula smirks, leans back, holds the box with his right arm and with his left arm, he quickly snatches out a hideous head. As the box drops, a white flash lights up the sky.

27

The Unbearable Sight

A hundred yards east from the souvenir shop, lays Henry. Roy drops to his knees and places his face on his neck. "Still alive." gasp Roy. Looking around, he spots two large rocks, grabs Henry under his arms and drags him behind the rocks. Roy quietly utters, "Never leave a soldier behind." and pats Henry's leg, as he gets up, and walks away.

He staggers back towards the souvenir shop and hears F-15 Eagle fighter jets thunder through the night sky, towards camp. The roar of an EC-130E Commando Solo plane descends on the base. He speaks under his breath, "There's too many of us in the sky." As he gets closer to camp, Roy moves from a limp to a fast walk. Less than a quarter of a mile to go, he sees what appear to be several thousand troops on the ground. His walk turns into a jog. His heart beats faster and faster as he closes in. The tower gives him three blue flashes; it's a message, which tells him that he is spotted.

He breathes extensively, not from jogging, but from the fear of what may have become of the camp. Less than three hundred yards, he sprints. A panting sound emits from his voice as he runs like hell; *anxieties a bitch*. When he arrives at the south side of the camp, two soldiers place their hands in the air and speak up, "You can't…" "Shut up." Roy interrupts. They realize his rank and allow him through.

Shocked, Roy walks through the camp. The smell of black powder and cooked flesh smothers; the rank smell of burnt skin and boiled blood turns his stomach. Roy's seen this sight before, but this time, he sees wolves; Hundreds upon hundreds are scattered all over the camp in piles. Splattered guts dangle from every sight. In terror, He begins to look for his men. Soldiers swarm, but not one is from his unit; it's the Hundred and First Division. This is the unit, which is called upon when there's high levels of combat. Roy figures there's at least fifteen hundred men on the ground. There's commotion in every direction. Men are carrying large wolves and stacking them in piles.

Roy grabs one of the privates arm, who's helping carry a dead wolf, "Private, First Lieutenant Ben U. Wynn, where is he?" "Sir, I don't know sir." "How about Second Lieutenant Tyler D. Smith?" "Sir, I don't know." "Well what the hell do you know private, do you know where any of the 82nd Division is?" "They're gone sir." "Gone?" He releases the privates' sleeve, and looks around speaking as he turns away, "What the fuck are you talking about, gone?" The private just looks puzzled, picks up his end of the wolf and continues his duty. Roy looks baffled and astonished as he wanders into the crowds of busy troopers. He walks toward the Sphinx and notices the line of tanks and downed helicopters. There's no external impact of missile fire on the choppers; there's no impact to the tanks. His eyes begin to focus inside one of the downed choppers. Inside, lays two piles of what looks like rocks. "What the hell?" Roy snaps into a stare, and looks up and around the camp. He sees it, piles of rocks all over the place.

The clumps of crystallized hardened white and grey ashy molds of warped sculpture sends mixed signals into his mind. Reasoning, he speaks out, "This shit wasn't here when I left." He walks over to several mounds of what appears as melted rocks. On one of the tanks, he spots a uniform. It's shredded and sticks out of a rock. He notices the gold bar. His heart races, Roy knows that it's Smiths uniform. "Ben." He turns and looks around, he's sure that Ben had to be near. Behind the tank stand several mounds of rock. His eyes begin to tear, as he walks slowly toward the mounds of rocks. His head begins to shake. "No, no man, naw." He walks up to a radio on the ground and traces the wire to the middle of the rock. Part of the last name can be made out, it's the letters NN; it's Ben's uniform. "Ben, Ben, Ben." Roy cries. He falls down on his knees, grabs, and hugs the mound. Letting out uncontrolled sighs, he loses himself, "No Ben, no Ben, you win man; Ben no, you win!"

Wailing is heard from one end of the camp to the other. Roy begins to peer around his surroundings. "What happened, shit, what is this?" Animal remains engulf; Canine brains, hair, and intestines are under his feet. The tanks are covered in blood. For as far as his eyes can see, there's melted figures. There's no sign of human remains, except the battered clothes molted within the mounds.

Roy shakes his head and begins to think of his youth when he played with plastic army men. He would get model car glue and matches and burn them until they melted. The smell of sulfur, gunpowder and burnt skin causes him to gag. He spits on the ground and cries out, "Fucking army men, melted army men." The side of Roy's face rubs against the remains of Ben, causing residue to stick to his face.

Exhausted, his dry mouth hangs open as he uses his right shoulder to rub the powdered remains off his cheek; he licks the corner of his mouth, only to taste salt. The salt's so strong that it makes his tongue raw. The nasty taste of the residue causes him to spit, but nothing comes out of his cottonmouth. Roy looks at Ben's remains, "That's salt." His eyes get big as he tries to blink the blur out of his sight. A long stare hits his face while he takes short breaths; he feels his own heart beat in his chest.

The scratchy voice of Major Thomas M. Scarborough is heard behind Roy, "Pick him up." Two soldiers grab him from the remains of Ben. He bows his head as the soldiers lift him under his arms. Roy stands, and is turned around facing Scarborough. He notices the gash on Roy's face and the wounds under his wrapped hands.

"Take him to the Medics." Dismayed, he looks up at Scarborough, drops his head, lets out a breath and passes out. The two soldiers carry Roy to the medical unit. The medics hook a heart monitor, administers I.V. into his right arm, as they sew up the deep gash on Roy's left cheek. They send report to the Major that Roy is to be transported for extensive surgery on his hands. He's unconscious and is transported aboard the Majors plane, the EC-130E Commando Solo.

Roy wakes up to the sound of a man and woman talking. They are nurses. She turns to the ruffling sound of his moving arm. "Oh, Captain

Johnson, nice of you to join us. How are you feeling?" Roy squints his eyes and questions her. "What time is it?" She lifts her arm, pulls her sleeve, and views her watch. "Well, let's see, it's six o five, evening." He squints his eyes and looks at her nametag. "What's today, um, nurse Brabson?" "Well ain't we all anxious to get up and go around here. Oh, and by the way, that's Major Brabson to you Captain." Roy comments back in a smart aleck way, "Excuse me sir. What makes me so special to get a Major to nurse me?"

"Well, I am the only one here qualified to clear your chart. I'm the chief nurse in this division." He looks at her full name, "It doesn't take a genius to figure that out, Major Missti D. Brabson. That's a cute name, Missti. Let me guess, the D stands for Denise?" "No, it stands for Deedra." He raises his eyebrows, "I should have known, Deedra. Well, at least the name goes with the face." "I hope that was a compliment Captain." "It was." says Roy in a high-pitched voice. "You're getting a little flirty, I'd better be going. Now, I will return in two hours to check your vitals again Captain." She turns and walks toward the door. "Sir, excuse me sir. You forgot to tell me what the day was sir." Missti turns. "It's Sunday. You still have time to watch football; it comes on at eight."

Missti grabs the remote on the television, walks to Roy, and hands him the remote. "By the way Captain, don't call me sir, call me Miss." "Yes Miss. And you don't have to call me Captain, call me Roy." "Okay Roy." She smiles, turns and walks out. He speaks under his breath, "Nice ass."

He hears a grunting sound and looks across the room; it's Henry. His eyes are shut, but Roy knows that he's not sleep. Henry's brow is hardened; Roy can sense the anger from him. The rooms quiet. He figures that he's mad at him for leaving a soldier down. He stares at him, hoping to catch him open his eyes. He speaks up, "I didn't mean to leave you, but I had to." He awaits a response, but there's not a sound. "Well, if you don't forgive me, I don't blame you. I'm not going to begin to make excuses. You were my best, and I didn't want harm to come to my best. Hell, you know I had to weigh the balance between one man and several. Well hell, you know the story." There's ten seconds of silence. Roy starts again, "Hell, I couldn't have carried you back if I tried."

Roy's sits up in his bed and faces Henry. "You wanna watch the game?" Still there's silence. He uses the remote and turns on the television. He doesn't notice Henry's eyes watching the television. Henry

31

mutters, "Sir, You saved my life." He presses the mute button; turning his head towards him, he speaks up, "What was that?" Henry clears his throat, "Sir, I'm not mad sir."

Roy looks and lets out a long breath, "Well, I am." Henry understood that Roy broke his golden rule, to never leave a soldier behind. He remembers how Roy would pound it in his head to always prioritize the importance of human life, especially that of your fellow company.

"Sir, permission to speak freely." Roy's eyes lock on Henry, who's still looking toward the television. "Permission granted." "They've kept you sedated the whole trip back. It wasn't until Major Brabson arrived that they would even allow you to come off the anesthesia. She kept you down since we arrived here at eighteen hundred hours Sunday."

"I watched the whole thing. They kept sticking you with needles. Hell, they had a hard time getting into your veins. They broke two needles on your arm. The funny part is, all this was going on, and you never bled once. They figured it had something to do with dehydration." Henrys face is puzzled. Roy knows that something else is bothering him. "What's really on your mind Specialist?" Henry knows Roy sees through his smoke screen when he calls him Specialist.

"Brigadier General Steve Marshall, Colonel Wade and Major Scarborough's been here three times. They were here this morning." Roy nods his head and speaks, "But that doesn't faze Henry. He has no fear, not even of his elders." "I've already swept the room for bugs." He acknowledges Henrys expertise. He un-mutes the television. Henry slowly springs out of bed, walks toward him and squats on one knee with his face next to his ear. Roy turns the volume up to muffle their conversation. Henry shakes his head, "What was it? It was too fast; before I could get a round off, bam, I was down. Hell, I didn't even know I was down. The next thing I remember is two medics asking me if I could move; Yeah, I felt fine. The whole way back, they were all looking at me like I was a ghost. I know what I saw, but they're not getting a word out of me." Roy looks at Henry, "The General huh?" "Yes sir." responds Henry. Roy nods his head yes. Henry gets up and returns to bed. Both of them know that they will have to keep it quiet for a while; it's just their way.

✳

Birth of Gargoyle

It's eight o'clock, Roy and Henry watch football. During the commercial break, a question mark comes over Roy's face, "What's our location?" Surprised, Henry answers, "You're home sir." "Home, Los Angeles?" "No sir, your other home, the place where you got your wings." Roy's dumbfounded, "Fort Bragg?" Henry smiles, "Fort Bragg North Carolina Womack Army Medical Center, fifth floor in the unnumbered room, south of the entrance to be exact sir."

"What the hell? Damn, I have been out for a while. That's one hell of a flight back." "Yes sir and they weren't kind enough to sedate me. I had to sit, and read the same sports magazine the whole way back. I read it so many times, that I practically have it memorized."

Ten minutes into the game, and in walks Major Missti D. Brabson. "Okay Captain Johnson, time for your stats." Roy raises his eyebrows and speaks in a monotone, "Good timing Major." "Oh, did I break up your little football party?" Roy looks at her butt, "No Miss, it's more like a tailgating party." Henry burst out a short chuckle.

"Oh, I see you want to be a comedian. Now be a good Captain and stick out your tongue." Roy holds his tongue out while Missti looks at his tonsils. "Good." She snaps a plastic cover on an electric thermometer and places it in his mouth. Now, let's get your blood pressure." Missti hands him a red ball with the 82nd Division's Emblem on it. "Now if you be a good little soldier, I'll let you keep this ball." Roy smiles while still holding the thermometer in his mouth. Missti touches his right arm. "Oh, you're cold; Are you okay?" Roy tries to speak without dropping the thermometer, "Yeah, I feel fine." "Well, your arms are freezing." Missti has him squeeze the rubber ball as she pumps the gauge. The sound of short beeps emits from the thermometer. "Okay, your blood pressure is normal. Missti releases the pressure and pulls the thermometer out of his mouth, and reads, "And your body temperatures normal."

Roy stares into Missti's eyes with curiosity, "Where did you go to school Major?" Surprised, Missti answers, "Well, I attended Harvard University for four years, and from there I attended Fort Sam Houston for a year, here at Womack another year, and then on to Walter Reed Medical Center for six years, where I worked at the Pentagon." "Oh, so you're from Boston?" "No, I didn't say I was from Boston." Roy nods his head, knowing that she'd never tell where's she from. He figures she still active with the Pentagon. Roy tones an upbeat expression, "So that's where you got to be Major, at the Pentagon." Missti quickly comments, "You're fishing in a dry pond soldier." Roy smiles, "Yeah, but I bet I could make that pond wet."

Missti bats her eyes at him, and lets out a soft breath, "Well, I have just one more thing for you Captain, and you and your colleague can finish the game." "Oh yeah." Roy remarks in a joking way. She steps out of the room. The sound of wheels squeaks as she returns with a scale on wheels. "Okay soldier, let's see you get up and we will see what you weigh." Roy gets out of bed and walks toward the door where Missti holds the scale. "Now the wheels lock, so you don't have to worry about the scale moving or anything." Roy speaks, "We wouldn't want that to happen, would we."

"Okay Captain Johnson, just step up and we will finish this all up for you." He questions, "So where's the usual weight and sliding bar you nurses use to weigh people?" Missti looks at the scale and points, "Well, this one is state of the art and it doesn't need a weight, because it can measure up to five hundred pounds." He responds, "Oh, I see."

Just as Roy begins to step onto the scale, Missti notices that she hadn't discarded the plastic cover on her electronic thermometer housed onto her waist. She turns and leans over the wastebasket to release the plastic cover. Roy steps onto the scale and notices the scale's gauge going around several times. He glances to see if Missti sees the gauge, but she's still turned. His heart begins to beat fast. He knows what he just saw. Missti turns around and looks at the scale, "Okay, let's see, you weigh two hundred and ten pounds, looks like you've gained twelve pounds."

Roy's eyes are big, he tries to reason to himself of what he just saw. "Captain, I said you can get off now." Startled, Roy snaps out of it, "Oh yeah." He steps off and the scale spins several times around counter clock ways. Missti writes on her chart and never notices. "So, this scale works?" "Why of course it works, do you want to go again?"

Roy quickly interjects, "No Miss, I believe you. I'm sure it works fine." Missti looks at him, "Well, I see you've put on a little weight. Maybe we should place you on our diet program here. You still look very fit; it's most likely muscle weight. You are very muscular you know?" "Thank you Miss." "Don't let that go to your head Captain." "Yes Miss. So we're done?" "Yes, we're done. Oh yeah, here." Missti hands him the rubber ball. Roy speaks in a suggestive manner, "Oh, thanks. I guess I can't say that you never gave me anything. So Major, when will we be able to get out of here?" Missti looks at her chart, "Looks like your party ends from here in the morning at o eight hundred. I'll still be here at o seven hundred to do my last routine check; and it looks like you can eat what you want too, so I will special order a big breakfast for the both of you." "Thanks Major." Roy smiles and gives her a firm handshake. As Missti turns, she begins to strut towards the door, "You boys don't stay up late at your tailgate party, because early comes early." "Yes Ma'am!" Roy solutes. "Yes Miss." speaks Henry, watching as she walks out. Roy turns to get back in bed, "Damn, now that's Major right there!" Henry laughs.

"Johnson?" Roy awakes to the sound of Missti's voice. Henry is already awake eating a hefty plate of sausage, eggs, gravy biscuits and pancakes. He focuses his view and notices the tray of food on the cart. "I know you have to be hungry honey. You want to sit up?" Roy lifts up in a sitting position, as Missti uses the remote to the bed to raise the head and back rest. "There you go. So how do you feel?" Without a word, Roy just nods his head yes. "Okay, let's see here." She shines a small

35

flashlight into his eyes to see his pupils. "Well, they're dilating." She checks his blood pressure and temperature which are both normal. "For your size, you are the healthiest soldier I've ever charted. Your blood levels are perfect, your cholesterol, well the whole nine yards." Roy's still adjusting his eyes to the morning sunrise, and just nod his head yes. Missti's puzzled, "Well aren't we the quiet one this morning. You want some breakfast?" Henry sops his biscuit, hoping Roy says no, so that he could eat his share. Roy gestures for the breakfast. She's baffled at his lack of reaction of her presence.

Missti adjust the cart and removes the cover, revealing the steamy food. "You want orange juice or milk?" "Water." "Water?" Missti hands him bottled water. Roy, nearly snatching it from her, immediately opens it and downs it in four long gulps. Her eyes are big. Roy catches himself acting like a barbarian, "I'm thirsty, you got some more water?" Missti blinks, "Sure." She hands him another water. He downs the water in under ten seconds. She shakes her head and smiles, "Well, at least I know your appetites back. Here, I am going to leave these other two waters here for you. Don't let your food get cold."

Henry speaks up, "Excuse me Major, but may I have the orange juice?" Missti walks over and hands the juice to Henry. "Looks like Johnson don't want it." Henry's delighted, "Thank you Major. Oh yeah, and thanks for the breakfast." Missti tilts her head and smiles, "You're welcomed soldier." She turns to say goodbye to a quiet Roy who's staring at his third bottle of water. Missti's offended; "Well don't let all that water spoil your breakfast soldier." Roy just looks up at her and shakes his head yes. Missti stands in front of his bed and stares at him. She's shocked that he's not flirting or even notices her. "Well, my times up, so long Smallback." She begins to walk toward the door, stops and glances back, "So long Roy." Roy's still looking at the bottled water. Henry speaks up, "Sir, aren't you going to thank the Major?" Roy blinks out of his stare, "Oh yeah, thanks Major."

Missti attempts one last try to get his attention, by saying his first name. "Okay Roy, I'll see you later on." He just nods yes, as his eyes are fixed on the bottled water. Missti walks out. Henry's offended, "Sir, if that was me and I had a woman that pretty give me the time of day, Major or not I'd be getting her phone number. Roy doesn't reply. Henry just shakes his head and looks at his tray, "Well, sir, are you going to eat that, because if you're not, I'd sure like to have it." "Sure, come and get it." Henry springs out of bed, with a big smile on his face; he happily pulls the cart over to his bed. Henry munches down. "Um, this is good. Thanks sir." "Oh, no problem man, I was just thirsty anyway." "Well sir, you're thirsty and I'm hungry; a perfect match." Roy downs the last bottle of water, "Yeah, I guess so."

The male nurse enters to take up the trays. He asks Roy if he wants him to remove the bandages from his hands. Roy speaks up, "How bad is it?" The nurse is puzzled, "What are you talking about sir?" Roy looks down and holds up his two bandaged hands. "My hands." "Well, I don't know why they bandaged your hands sir." "Didn't you do surgery? My fucking hands soldier, they're blistering." "Well, let's take a look sir." As the nurse goes to unwrap one of his bandages, Roy pulls back, "Hey, be careful." The nurse unwinds the bandage from Roy's left hand. Roy's eyes grow big with anticipation of the damage. As his hand begins to show, he sees nothing. There are no burns or scars. He hurry's the nurse, "Check my right hand." The nurse unwraps his other hand revealing perfect hands.

Roy notices the scar on his right wrist. "Hey, what about this scar?" The nurse shuns, "What about it sir?" "Don't' get smart with me soldier, I'll have your ass. How did this scar get here?" The nurse thinks he's paranoid. "Sir, I don't know where you got that scar; perhaps when you were a kid or something. That scar looks like it's been there for years. Maybe it was a bicycle accident when you were a kid, or a fight you got into as a child." The nurse gets up; He wants to get out of the room. "What about my ear?" He turns, "Excuse me sir?" "My ear, you need to check my ear."

The nurse looks into Roy's ears, "Well, they both look good to me and your charts check out just fine. There's even a note here sir that your ears are exceptionally clean for a soldier who just came from the desert sir." "What?" Roy snatches the chart from the nurse and reads through several pages. There are several notes as to the perfect health he was in. All stats were one hundred percent; some were noted a hundred and ten percent. Roy calms down, looks at the nurse, and hands him the chart. "I guess I was a little paranoid, I lost my men in battle. Carry on soldier, thanks." The nurse gets up and salutes, "It's been a pleasure to meet you sir, have a great day." Roy looks over the nurses' shoulder. It's Major

Thomas M. Scarborough, standing. Roy speaks to the nurse, "Okay soldier, you're dismissed." Scarborough's holding two uniforms and a bag with shoes. "Boy's get dressed; you're out of here at o eight hundred, that gives you twenty minutes. They both get dressed. Roy gives Henry the look; they both know what's next. "You know how to act Specialist." "I learned from the best sir."

Roy approves, "I'm proud of you son, I'll see to it that you get what you want." Henry raises his brow, "I'd like to be back in action sir." "I know you do Specialist." "You deserve the Purple Heart; I'll see to it that you get what you've earned. You were obeying orders as usual, got it?" Henry smiles, "Yes sir." Roy, patting his shoulder, speaks, "Lets get out of here."

Henry opens the door where stands Major Scarborough and two MPs. Roy follows behind, he knows something's fishy going on with two MPs escorting them. Scarborough speaks up, "Gentlemen, you look great." They solute him. "At ease soldiers. I'm taking you guys to headquarters for debriefing; Follow me." Roy and Henry walks with Scarborough towards the elevators. With no luck, Roy looks around to see if he could spot Missti, he wants to officially tell her thanks.

When they reach the elevators, Roy feels an unusual amount of energy, much like an adrenaline rush. They all step onto the elevator. As the doors shut, the elevator light flashes with a buzzard sound. It shows that the elevator is overloaded and has too much weight. The doors open as Scarborough steps out and lashes, "What the hell's going on with this junk? Nurse, what's wrong with this elevator?" A nurse heads over and looks at the elevator, "I don't know sir; it was working here a while ago." "Well hell, I know that, but it's not working now, It says that it's reached over maximum capacity, And I sure the hell know that the five of us don't weigh over two thousand pounds." "Sir I don't know." Well you'd better call maintenance to fix it." Scarborough looks at the soldiers, "Gentlemen let's take the stairs."

As they begin to go down the stairs, Roy notices his boots soles were giving in to his weight. Each stairwell begins to make a creaking sound as they descended. Roy didn't want to draw attention to himself, so he moved as hastily as he could behind the Major. They all load into a Hummer and head for headquarters. The Hummer stops and the two MP's jump out. Scarborough speaks, "You're going with them

Smallback." "Yes sir." Henry jumps out and is escorted into a small brick building.

Two buildings down, is headquarters. The driver gets out and opens the door for the Major and Roy. The Major steps out first. "Well Captain, lets get this over with." Roy jumps out, places his cap on and follows Scarborough into headquarters.

After a long walk through headquarters, Scarborough opens the door to the private sectors room; this is the place, where only high-ranking officers are allowed. As Roy steps in, There awaits Colonel Reginald E. Wade, and Lieutenant Colonel Bradley N. McDouglas. From that day, Roy and Henry experience five days of the most strenuous moments of their entire military career. The questions last eight hours, with one hour lunch breaks. They both are escorted to separate isolated rooms, with no telephones or televisions.

On that Thursday, Roy and Henry are placed into the same room, across from the private sectors door. They are asked the same questions to see if their stories match. Major Thomas M. Scarborough, Colonel Reginald E. Wade, and Lieutenant Colonel Bradley N. McDouglas drill them six hours straight.

Lieutenant Colonel McDouglas questions Henry, "What were you doing exactly at twenty three hundred hours that Saturday?" "I was posted outside the souvenir shop." "And how did you get to the point behind the rocks?" "I don't know sir; the next thing I remember is waking up to two medics who transported me to camp." Henry and Roy never look at each other during debriefing.

Roy smirks to himself, he's proud that Henry follows his training when he is interrogated. McDouglas looks at Roy, "And what are you smiling at Captain?" "Sir, I was smiling, because you've asked this question over ten times in the last hour." McDouglas interrupts, "Captain, If I want to ask the same question a thousand times in one hour, then I have that right; Don't you ever question me again, you hear?" Roy gives a serious look, "Sir, Yes sir." Both Henry's and Roy's stories match. Colonel Wade, the original person who helped enlist Roy, speaks to him, "Johnson, is this how it all happened?" Wade knows that Roy is one of his best and is a very honorable person. He responds "Sir, yes sir." Wade looks deep into Roy's eyes and looks at McDouglas, "he's telling the truth." McDouglas begins to gripe, but Wade interrupts him, "I said that was all Lieutenant. Okay, this session resumes in one hour."

In the mess hall, Roy and Henry face each other. Scarborough sits next to Roy and speaks, "Damn Johnson, that's four days and I've not seen you eat a thing." Roy looks with seriousness. "This bottled water will do me just fine Major." "Listen, don't you think I don't like this? Well I don't." Roy continues drinking with a serious look. "Well, finish up boys; we have two more hours of this." The Major gets up and hands his tray to a soldier who's walking by. Roy looks at Henry, "I'm proud of you." Henry smiles, "Well I've learned from the best." "Well Specialist, let's get this crap over with. We have a long day ahead of us tomorrow, and we'd better get all the rest we can tonight." Henry shakes his head, "Yeah, it sucks not having a TV."

On Friday at ten hundred hours, Roy is escorted back into the private sectors quarters. He solutes Scarborough, who enters in alone. "At ease; now listen Johnson, you and I have known each other for ten years now. You know me, hell; I'm doing all I can to make this easy on you, Henry and myself. Now it's just you and me, nobody else. Tell me what really happened. I'm granting you permission to speak whatever is on your mind, okay?" Roy waits a half of minute. Scarborough's hoping that he can shake what's going on in Roy's mind. Roy sits down, "Okay sir." "Good." Scarborough sits down facing him. "Well, everything happened just the way we told you. I was the one who moved Smallback behind those rocks; He was unconscious."

Scarborough interrupts, "You left your men; you knew your orders." "Come on Thomas, don't bullshit me, it's not about me leaving my men; you and I know that it was routine for me to go out there." "But why did you go there, you guys already had enough beer; Hell even the girls." "We saw a light." "Come on Johnson, I've already heard this one from Henry a thousand times." "It's the truth man." "You mean to tell me that you guys had to go and see a flashlight from a shop that sells flash lights? Well, why couldn't you send out scouts if you thought that a flash light was so damned important?" Roy defends, "It wasn't that kind of light sir." "Well what kind of light was it Johnson, a lighting bug, a strobe light?" "No sir, it was more like lightning flashing." Scarborough is dismayed at Roy's explanations, "Are you fucking kidding me? There wasn't a cloud or storm within thousands of miles of your location. The only storm headed your way was a small dust storm, which is normal for this time of the year, so don't give me that, you saw a light bulb cockamamie story."

Roy, furious, "So what the hell are you saying here Thomas; Are you saying that you wished I was back at the base, then everything would have been alright, huh?" Scarborough realizes he crossed the line. "Hey, I didn't mean it like that." "So what do you mean, cause from my view point, you're mad that I wasn't at the camp." Scarborough nods his head no. "And since we are back on the subject of the camp, I want to know a few things; what the hell were we protecting, and why were there splattered dog shit all over the camp? Where in the hell did we get the money for silver ammo? Are you trying to tell me that we were protecting Little Red Riding Hood and a bunch of big bad wolves came to get her?" Scarborough's eyes light up; quiet, he has a guilty look on his face.

Roy catches himself in the phrase and ponders what he just said. "What did I say that hit your nerve Major, huh?" The Major sits back, lets out a hard breath, pushes his chair back and stands. "The General's on his way, he wants to talk to you." Roy's surprised, "To me, for what?" "I'm leaving you here to think until the General arrives." Scarborough turns and shuts the door behind him quietly.

Roy knows that it's really serious when the General gets involved in any debriefing matters. While he waits, he begins to wonder about his words. He's curious why they'd use antifreeze infused into their ammunition. It all seems like a make believe horror story. The clock on the wall seems to move slowly as molasses. Roy looks at his hands; they were not shaking as usual. He feels his body; it dawns on him that he's not perspired or sweated through the whole debriefing process. He's forgotten to cry; He doesn't feel the pain that you are supposed to feel when something deer to you is lost. He looks up at the fluorescent lights in the ceiling. Instead of hurting his eyes, they look very dim to him; the room seems dark. Roy gets up, walks to the window, and looks outside. The sun is bright and there's not a cloud in the sky; but somehow, gloom fills the room; it feels dark. He thinks to himself that he must be experiencing shock from the lost of his best friend and his men.

Six hours pass, and in walks Scarborough followed by Brigadier General Steve C. Marshall. Roy jumps up and solutes. "At ease Johnson." speaks the General. "Be seated son." The General sits down while Scarborough stands. "Johnson, what's this malarkey about you not eating?" Roy looks down, "I'm just not hungry sir." "Well I am, and you need to eat, so I am ordering you to lunch, and that's an order." Roy looks up, "Yes sir." The General looks at Scarborough, "And that's without escorts; you get that Major?" "Yes sir." The General checks his watch, "This briefing will resume at nineteen hundred." He stands and walks out. Roy stands and salutes. The Major looks at him, "Well you heard the General, Go get some food." "Yes sir." Scarborough walks out, leaving the door open.

Roy walks out the door and shuts it behind him. There are no soldiers in sight. In great respect for the General, Roy heads for the mess hall. He orders himself an apple with corn, a salad and a hamburger, along with orange juice. As he eats, Roy has an awful taste in his mouth. He can taste the blood from the burger, the can from the orange juice and the insecticide in the fruit and salad. Roy finishes his meal, but feels sick to his stomach. Looking at the clock, he realizes that it took him a whole hour to down a simple meal. He quickly rushes a private to drive him back to headquarters. Roy's ten minutes late, something he's never done in the history of his career. He comes to the door, takes off his cap and walks in the room, where waits the General and Scarborough. The General stands as Roy salutes, "Please be seated son."

The General looks and speaks to Scarborough, "Step outside." Shocked, Scarborough starts, "But!" "No questions son." he interrupts. "Yes sir." Scarborough closes the door behind him. The General has a peaceful look on his face and begins to explain why Roy was brought into the mission. "Son, there was valuable merchandise in that Sphinx, and someone got to it. But it's not your fault; I should have been there myself. Hell, it was my full intention on having a full division present. I just didn't make it in time, that's all. You are one of my best, I mean, I was hoping that one day." The General chokes up. "You remind me of me when I was your age. Damn, you're like a son to me. I am so sorry that you lost your men in operation KEEP OUT. If I could go back, I would."

Roy picks up that more is going on in the Generals mind than what he displays. He asks, "Sir, What were those dogs and what were those rocks?" The General answers softly, "They were timber wolves. Hell, it appears that the terrorist trained these dogs to attack our soldiers. Roy interrupts, "And the bullets?" "I ordered those bullets; the chemical would serve in a sure way just in case some dogs escaped with gun wounds.

The poison antifreeze crystallizes the blood and, well you know what that does son. The rocks, well, I can't explain that. It appears that the terrorist used some sort of weapon of mass destruction, which instantly burned and carbonized our men. Any more questions?" Roy drops his head, "No sir."

The General calls Scarborough back into the room. "Now, the information disclosed in this debriefing in its entirety is classified. He looks to Scarborough, "You have my paper work?" "Yes sir." Scarborough hands him a manila folder. The General signs the forms. Now Johnson, I am ordering you on vacation." The General stands, walks around to Roy. He salutes the General, but the General places his hand out for a shake. Roy shakes his hand. With a tearful voice the General speaks, "It's been a great pleasure son." The General turns looks at Scarborough and walks out. Scarborough looks at Roy, "Have a seat Johnson, I'll be back." Roy sits.

Scarborough returns, "Please keep your seat Johnson." Sitting down he opens the manila folder and begins to write. Roy anticipates that it will be a two or three week vacation release form. Scarborough takes the forms out and hands them to Roy. He smiles and looks at the top form. His smile turns into disappointment as he looks up at Scarborough, "Hey what the hell is this, this is a DD two fifty six A." He looks at the second form; it's a certificate with the General, Wades and Scarborough's signatures. "An honorable discharge, what the hell is this for?" Scarborough interjects, "Now Johnson, I've managed to pull some strings for you; Hell, I've busted my ass to get you this package. Roy's hostile, "This is a Goddamn joke!" Scarborough continues, Now Johnson, I've managed to get you full medical and dental, I mean you pay nothing, now that's something very few ever see." "So all this debriefing bullshit was just a smoke screen to knock me off the fucking planet? I thought you were my Major; above that, I thought you were my friend, Thomas."

"I am your friend Roy! Do you think I wanted this, well the answers no. Believe me, I tried everything to keep them from this, but I just don't' have that power. Now if you know what's good for you, you'd sign this." Roy looks into his eyes. He sees Scarborough's pain, and then looks down at the forms. "Now we managed to get you a departing pay of two hundred with monthly pay of twenty."

Roy begins to glance at the forms in disappointment and looks up at Scarborough, "Are you kidding me, two hundred dollars, and twenty dollars a month, that's a joke." Scarborough squints his eyes at him, "That's two hundred g's with a pay of twenty thousand a month; that's more than any Generals made around here. It is a considerable amount to receive and you'd be a fool not to take it Johnson." "Oh I see, its hush hush money." "No Johnson, you earned it and you and I know that you and your men were worth every penny of it. Besides, you never knew the danger you were going into as was the case with most your missions." Roy shakes his head negatively, "What about Henry?" "He's active after three weeks and I'll make sure that he gets his promotion and the Purple Heart just as you requested." "How do I know that I can believe you Major?" Scarborough reasons, "Listen Johnson, you are welcomed here at anytime as visiting veteran, and I'd be glad to have you for lunch any day. As for Henry, well you can talk to him whenever you need to; He flies out tomorrow."

Roy signs the forms, and looks Scarborough in the eye. Scarborough separates his copies, stands and places his hand out, "Now you take care." Roy pushes himself away from the table and rises to shake his hand. Scarborough pulls him close and hugs him. "I'll miss you Johnson." Scarborough's eyes are red as he holds back tears. Roy never cries, but he feels the emotion. Scarborough stands back and salutes Roy one last time, "To the Captain who deserves to be called Major." Roy solutes back. Scarborough pivots and walks out the door. Roy's alone, he feels physically weak. He slowly grabs his papers and places them into his folder. He walks out and shuts the door behind him. Walking out, he notices the MP at a jeep. "Excuse me, could you tell me where they have Smallback?" The MP points, "Yes sir, he's in that building down there. Do you need a ride?" "No Thanks, I'll walk; and thank you for the information."

Roy walks towards the small brick building. As he begins to get closer to the building, he feels dizzy. Henry's looking out the window and sees Roy approaching. A smile comes over Henry's face. He quickly packs the rest of his stuff and heads towards the door. Before Roy knocks on the front door, Henry greets him with a salute. "Sir, how's it going?" "Well hell, I see you are ready to get out of here Specialist." Henry looks back at his duffle bag. "Yes sir, I'm packing, want you come in?" Roy goes in behind Henry. "Oh hell, this is a small unit." "Yeah, but at least I got to watch television last night." "Oh really?" "Yeah, I even got to catch up on

44

some fishing tips on cable."

Henry looks in Roy's hands, "Oh, I see they gave you your papers too. They gave me three weeks vacation, with pay and a twenty one hundred dollar bonus. The General just left and he gave me this." Henry shows him the Purple Heart. "I know you had something to do with that sir. Well, I just want to say, thanks." "Hell, don't thank me Specialist, thank yourself, because you've earned it." Henry smiles, "I was going to stay till the morning just to meet you, but you're here now. I wanted to make sure that everything was all right and that I got a chance to see you sir. Well, now you're here, I guess I can go now." Roy smiles at Henry, "That would be a great idea Specialist." Henry questions, "So how long did they give you?" He looks down at his folder, "Oh, they gave me a long vacation." He laughs, "That's good sir." Roy shakes his hand. Henry, never big on showing emotion, sternly speaks, "Thanks for saving my neck sir."

Roy has a pale look; Henry watches, "Are you alright sir?" his stomach begins to heave, "Oh, I feel sick at my stomach. I think I ate a bad burger." Henry speaks up, "It's probably from not eating for so many days sir. Well, anyway, if you have to barf, there's a bathroom right there." Henry salutes Roy, "Well sir, I will see you around on our next mission." Roy nods, "Yeah, take care." Henry carries his duffle bag out, and leaves the door open.

Roy's eyes follow as Henry fades into the dusk horizon. He immediately turns and runs to the bathroom. He has never felt so much pain in all his life. The awful feeling causes him to vomit into the toilet. For ten minutes, Roy experiences a torture he's never felt before. After several flushes, he looks up at the mirror; His eyes have a bluish haze to them. He blinks them, adjusting to the lights inside; it seems so dark.

Roy feels around his stomach, it seems like he was never sick; there's shock of his quick recovery. As he begins to go out, he looks down and sees his footprints indented into the hardwood floor. This takes him for another spin as he glances down at his shoes; the soles are worn completely down.

Roy stands at the bathroom entrance and looks up at the trail he's made. As he walks, the floor begins to make a loud creaking sound. The wood arches downward giving way to Roy's weight; He hurries out the door. He wonders what's going on with his body. Remembering the scale and the elevator at Womack, he quickly begins towards a nearby supply warehouse. Roy's used the warehouse on several occasions. At the warehouse, his own unit greets him. They notice who he is and solutes him. "Captain Sir." "At ease soldier, I just came here to weigh myself." "Sir, well, we don't have a regular scale sir." "I know that soldier, but I know that at least this scale works. The nurse at Womack said I weighed over two hundred pounds and I know that's not right." The soldier laughs, "Well, sure, if you want to, you know where it is over there." Roy walks over to the scale. The scale is used for weighing heavy equipment and artillery. He looks behind himself to make sure the soldier doesn't notice.

Roy hardens his face, takes a deep breath and steps on the scale. There are two readings, one is digital and the other is mechanical; He looks at both. The scale continues past two hundred pounds and stops at twenty one hundred pounds. Roy's astounded. He steps off and steps back on the scale, which reads again at twenty one hundred pounds. The soldier yells over, "So how much you weigh sir?" Roy steps off the scale and scatters for an answer, "Oh, she was right, I did gain weight." He starts out, "Thanks." "Yes sir." solutes the soldier who scrambles and calls, "Oh yeah, sir, are you going to pick up your storage tonight or in the morning?" Roy turns, "My storage is here?" "Yes sir." The soldier walks over to the storage and unlocks the cabinet, revealing his personals from Egypt. The soldier hands them to him. "Oh yeah my watch and my collections." He holds up his nine millimeter. "Hell, I forgot all about this stuff."

The soldier unlocks a large cabinet where hangs several assault rifles and pulls out a long dark object. He lays it on the counter and pulls back a blanket, revealing the sword from the souvenir shop. "Well, I managed to clean off all the sand and polish it.

I tried to clean the blade, but it wouldn't come out. It must be welded or jammed, so I left it alone, because I didn't want to break it sir." Roy looks on the floor behind the soldier. "Hey, do you need that gun case?" "Sir, no sir." "May I have it?" "Yes sir." as he squats, lifts the army green rifle case, and hands it over. Roy recovers the sword and places it in the case. His eyes light up as he looks at the soldiers name tag, he appreciates, "Thanks, Private First Class Phelps." "Yes sir." salutes the private.

Roy heads back towards his bunk. He ponders the uncanny way that he was able to get all his stuff back. When he gets to his location, he opens the door and places the case and personals on the desk. His heart jumps as he glances around at the bed, he speaks, "Why the hell didn't the bed break?" He walks to the shower, "This tile should have cracked". When he turns and looks into the full mirror, he notices his arms. They are more muscular than he's ever seen them. He pulls his shirt off, revealing the definition of his torso. "Who the hell is this?" Ecstatic, he quickly strips down nude, revealing the massive definition of his body. He scrambles his thoughts and looks for an explanation behind his muscular tone, "Hell, I know I'm in shape but this is insane." He begins to count back days and comes to an eye awakening experience, "I've not had anything to eat in five days. I'm not even hungry or weak at all." Roy realizes that something mysterious has happened to him. He begins to reason in his mind, but all he wants to do is get to his home in Los Angeles. He quickly pulls his mattress off his bed and places it on the floor. He wants to make sure that he doesn't leave any evidence of his bodies chemistry change. He realizes that he will fly back to Los Angeles on the EC-130E Commando Solo and is sure it will be able to support his weight. He figures that He will just sit in the cargo area by request.

Roy sleeps, and dreams he's a creature who orders demons to kill certain people. The people are usually known for a notorious act, which sends Roy on a hunt to kill them. Sometimes He orders demons to kill, and other times when the person is very strong, he does the job himself. He seeks to destroy a tall man in all black wearing a cape. The town of London hires witches to place a curse on him, but it doesn't work, so they bring cats to attack him. He chases the man in black, but is headed off by an old white and gray haired man in a long blue trench coat, holding a gray cat.

As Roy crosses a bridge walkway, the old man tells the cats to jump him.

Two cats attack him, one from behind and the other in front; the yellow cat jumps his back and the white jumps at his legs. He crushes the yellow cats' skull and goes for the white cat. At that moment, several thousand cats jump him. He knows he's fast, but he's not sure if he can kill all the cats that claw into his flesh.

Roy realizes that he's only dreaming, but thinks to himself that if he only focuses his eyes a certain way, then he could see it. He opens his eyes and notices a large head looking over him. A lion like creature wearing a helmet with a facemask is watching him. It appears as some sort of space gear, which covers the outer rim of the lions face, nose and mouth.

Surprised that he wakes, the lion face creature panics and turns away while looking back at Roy. He's not able to hear the lion breathe, but he sees it breathing rapidly. He watches, only to see the lion head fade into the dark. Glancing over at the alarm clock on the dresser, it's three in the morning. He waits to see if the creature would appear again. He turns and speaks, "Three fifteen." He gets out of bed and realizes he had a wide-awake vision. "That's never happened before, was that real?" Roy has heard of people sleep walking, but this is his first experience of anything on that level.

Roy attempts to lie down and sleep, but begins to rationalize why he just saw what he did. He talks to himself, "There's no way I was sleep when I saw that thing. Maybe I only thought I saw it, but if that's true, then why did it get surprised when I rose up and looked at it? Okay, why did I dream about cats?" He talks it out, "Damn, It actually felt like I could feel those cats clawing me. It felt real, but when I woke up, this massive lion head's caught getting some kind of thrill off of my pain, but when I woke out of it, the thing was surprised I could see." Being sure that he was one hundred percent awake, Roy concludes that his brain tricked him into seeing what he saw. He still has a little doubt, because he's not able to figure why the creature would panic and disappear. He gets up and takes a shower. While in the shower he has a strong thought that teaches him that there's someone who gets there kicks off watching others. He thinks of the Sphinx and the Egyptians who believed in lion like creatures. The joy of the warm water is interrupted by a cracking sound under his feet. While the shower runs, he quickly steps out and looks at the floor; one tile is cracked. He decides to finish his wash by using the sink.

Roy dries off and slips on his clothes. He examines his worn shoes and puts them on. Getting up from the floor, he sits in a metal chair that holds his weight. As he sits at the desk, he glances up to see the night and the lights from the streets. Roy takes a second look. He can see small particles floating in the air; He is able to make out every detail of the particles. He focuses his eyes towards the light in the bathroom and sees several red, blue, and white particles move rapidly. The particles are all over the room. He looks all around and stops to focus on his mouth, which breathes them in and out. Some are in clusters, but most bounce in every direction. He doesn't realize that he sees molecules and atoms.

Standing up, he walks to the bathroom, reaches over and turns out the light. When the light goes out, Roy's eyes begins to shine blue. Roy stares at his reflection. He walks towards the mirror and touches his face and then the mirror to make sure that it was there. "I'm not dreaming; this is real. Why ain't I scared? I should be running out of my damned mind right now; what the hell am I?"

Roy, in awe of his presence, has no fear of what he's become. He stands in the mirror and gazes until the sunrise. When the sun comes up, his eyes are bright amber. It feels natural for him. The alarm clock goes off; it's time for departure to Los Angeles. A good feeling comes over him as he walks out and closes the door. At o eight hundred, he boards the EC-130E Commando Solo and heads for California. He's happy and feels good that he's witnessed something amazing; a new man is born.

✳

Demon Stalkers

The big melting pot, Los Angeles California is recorded as one of the largest cities in the nation. This is the city where you can find every imaginable person possible. Roy lands at LAX at two in the afternoon. Out of the cargo bay, he steps onto the airport runway where waits a transport vehicle to take him to the front of the airport. He steps out of the transport vehicle and grabs his luggage and gun case. As he walks to find a suitable cab, he's approached by an old smelly man who appears to wear two toboggans, four shirts, two old nasty blue jeans and brown dress shoes with the toes worn out. "Got a quarter?" "Hell no, I don't have a quarter." Roy walks past the old man. He stops and thinks about what he just did, reaches in his pocket and pulls out two dollars. He turns to hand the old man the two dollars, but doesn't see him.

Roy looks at the waiting taxi, and tells him to go ahead. He scans the crowds to find the old man. Over there, he stands next to a woman who also appears to be a street person. As Roy approaches, he notices that the woman is arguing at the wall behind the old man. Roy squints his eyes, "She's out of her fucking mind." He taps the old man on the back and hands him the two dollars. The old man's eyes brightens up, "Thank you, mommas got your money in the bank." Roy nods his head yes. He's not sure what the old man meant, but starts to walk off. The old lady gets louder; she's still going off at the wall.

As Roy begins to walk away, he hears the woman speak "You fucking asshole don't come over here with that crap!" Roy hears a lisping voice of a man saying, "Shut up, don't look at him." The sound makes Roy's ears ring. His eyes begin to turn a brighter amber color. He smells stink, but he also smells a metallic substance; it almost smells like rusted metal. He turns and looks at the woman who's still facing the wall as she gets louder, "What are you looking at, are you scared?" Roy thinks the lady is talking to him, but wonders how she'd know he was looking at her with her back facing him.

Roy starts toward the old lady who screams out, "Where?" She turns and looks at Roy and talks out the corner of her mouth, towards the wall, "You afraid?" When he walks up to the old woman, she turns and yells at the wall, "You fucking asshole, don't be scared!" Roy really thinks she's lost it and stops to walk back, but something catches his eye. He starts closer and hears, "You come to kill me?" His eyes get big; it's a dark shadow on the wall. "What the fuck?" The shadows black eyes get big and speaks again, "Asim, you come to kill me before my time?" Roy stands next to the old lady and sees the hideous deformed shadow. It looks like a naked man, translucent like smoke from tar. The lady curses Roy, but he ignores her. The shadow begins, "I thought you were no more; please allow me to pass." As Roy approaches, the shadow lets out a loud shrill and flies away. "Look what you've done, you've scared him off." rants the old lady. Roy looks at her, and smells a horrible scent of blood from the lady. He sees her aura, which emits dark red. As he walks away from her, she hisses and spits, but Roy's too far, as he fades into the crowd of busy people.

Roy gets a taxi and goes to his two-bedroom apartment on Arlington Street, just south of Hollywood California. Five o'clock that afternoon, he steps out of the cab and pays the driver. He looks up at his place, speaking, "Home." Suddenly he thinks to himself why he was able to ride in the transport vehicle and the cab without breaking the axles. He picks up his bags and gun case, presses his entrance code and goes into his apartment on the second floor. There are only four units. Across the hall lives an old lady and her white Siamese cat, while down stairs lives a Hispanic family of five and directly below him the apartment is vacant. Roy steps inside his apartment. He sets his bags down and lays his gun case on the coffee table. He's happy to be back. He looks down at his marble floor and thinks of the structure of the building. "Well, at least this place will hold my weight." Roy remembers picking the apartment complex because of its design of a small castle and safety bulletproof windows. Although the building looks new, its structure is over a hundred years old and is made of stone and marble. He steps into his bathroom and speaks up, "I'm getting a better shower and tub." While unpacking his bags Roy hears the message on his answering machine, it's Mrs. Randall the Landlord. "Mr. Johnson, when you get this message, it is very urgent that you call me."

Roy heart beats fast, as he observes that the answering machine wasn't running. "How the hell?" Roy takes a second look and hears the message again, but the tapes not running. He quickly scrambles to rewind and play the tape. He presses play, "Mr. Johnson, when you get this message, it is very urgent that you call me." A blank stare falls on his face as he sits down on the floor in shock. Before he gathers another thought, he picks up the phone before it rings; it's Mrs. Randall. "Hello?" she inquires. He answers, "Hello?" "Is this you Mr. Johnson?" "Yes." "Well, I was just calling you, but I never heard it ring on my end." He thinks quickly, "Oh, I was just getting ready to make a call and I guess I picked up before it had a chance." The lady excites, "Well, ain't that something. I've tried to call that number you gave me from the Army, but they said you were out of town. I asked your neighbor Mr. Gonzales to call me when he saw you. So, did you get my letter?" "No ma'am, I just got in, and the post office is closed; they're holding my mail for me." "Well, I'm going to come out and tell you now that I'm sorry to inform you that I am selling the complex." Roy, in shock, speaks, "What, but why?" "I'm getting too old to keep the place up. Seems like every time I turn around, I'm paying taxes or they're raising taxes on me, so I've thought it out for a year and I've decided to let the place go. Now, I've given everyone six months, but you've been gone for five months."

Mrs. Randall begins to give Roy the details on how he can pick up his safety deposit, which includes a credit for moving expenses. "Wait a minute, this place goes way back, it has a lot of good history, surely

52

you don't want to get rid of your heritage? Hell, I'll even help you pay the taxes on it." "You don't understand Mr. Johnson, I'm just tired and I don't want to deal with it anymore." "Well May I ask how much you're selling it for?" "That's none of your business." "And why not, I might want to buy it." "If you think you have eighth million dollars, then you can have it." "Is that what you're selling it for, eight million?" She hurries him, "I'm through with this conversation."

Mrs. Randall starts to hang up her phone, but is interrupted by an anxious Roy, "Wait, wait, don't hang up just yet Mrs. Randall. You're right, I don't have eight million dollars, but I am sure I can get the loan from my bank, if you'd just give me the chance." "Well, I'm sorry Mr. Johnson, but I already have a buyer, and they are taking this place in six weeks." "Did you sign any papers, I mean, did you close the deal?" "Monday, I'm going on Monday."

Roy interjects "No, don't do it; Let me buy it." She nods her head, "I've already told them that they can have it, and besides, there's no promise that you're going to get the loan. You can't expect me to turn down a sure deal." Roy bargains, "Ten million." Mrs. Randall makes sure what she just heard, "What was that?" "They're buying it for eight million, so I'll buy it for ten." She hesitates, "I can't do that." Roy's voice squeaks, "And why not?" "One, I have to give them a month in advance before I vacate, and two, you don't have the money." "Give me two weeks." "I can't do that." "Well, give me one week then, and I promise you won't be disappointed. You give me a week, and if they want to buy it for more then what I'm buying it for, then there you have it; you would have made a bigger profit than what you originally asked."

Mrs. Randall really likes Roy and thinks it over. She's sure he'd take good care of the place. Money hungry, she gives him an answer, "Okay Mr. Johnson, I am giving you a week." Roy smiles, "Thank you Mrs. Randall. I'll call you in a few days okay?" She hesitatingly speaks, "Okay." she hangs up. He calls his broker and faxes copies of the pay rate from his retirement plan. After an hour of negotiating, his broker returns his call at seven with an approval based upon his promise, to place a down payment of two hundred thousand dollars. It will take five business days to complete the transactions, but the stamp of approval is sealed by the banks President. Roy feels good, he knows he can live off the fifty thousand dollars he has saved in the bank; He also knows that in six weeks, that he will be receiving his payments from the military.

The night is young but the day has just begun. Connie the prostitute is known for her high dollar tricks. Her southern bell appearance of innocence is used to lure the most noblest of men. Wearing a short mink jacket and a knee length dark red dress, she steps out of the black limo, reaches her head into the window, and kisses a man in white fur. As she pulls her head back, her hand falls to his outreached arm. She begins to rub her face on his fluffy white fox fur, and licks his index finger, which holds a large diamond. The man speaks, "This is your night." She places his finger into her mouth and sensually sucks it. The man pulls his arm back, "Naughty naughty." She smiles and pulls away, and turns to walk to the other side of the corner, while licking the blood off the corner of her mouth.

The chauffer looks back at the man, "I can't believe she bit you sir." While rolling up the window, the man gives the chauffer a snarl, "Never mind that, drive on." The sound of the gas accelerates as the limo speeds off. Connie pulls out a small mirror and applies fresh red lipstick on her full lips. Squeaking breaks are heard at the bus stop across the street; it's the Metro Rapid; a public transit that has made its last stop. Off steps the apostolic priest. He wears a hat and long coat. As the bus pulls off, he stands and looks down the street.

The priest hears a whistle; it's Connie across the street. A smile comes across the priest's face as he walks toward her. She seductively bats her eyes as he stops in front of her, "Hello Reverend." The priest looks to the left and right to see if anyone over heard her. "I told you not to say that." She pucks her lips, "Awe come on honey, have a sense of humor." "Well, we've discussed this before." She softly touches his chest and interrupts "Awe honey, be a good sport, I didn't mean any harm." The priest nods, "Well, okay, but please don't act like that." Looking innocent, she speaks, "Okay baby, I'm sorry, I won't ever do it again, I promise." The priest smiles, "Alright then. So, where's your limousine?" "Oh, well, I thought we'd walk tonight." "Walk?" "Yes, it so nice out tonight and besides, I have the perfect little spot for us just four blocks from here." "Oh really?" Connie embraces his arm as they walk together down the sidewalk.

One block from their point, it crawls down from the tree and follows. Connie places her head on the priest's shoulder and looks out the corner of her eyes behind him. She sees the red eyes as they hide behind the building. She lifts her head, "Let's stop here." The priest looks around, "How come?" She points behind him, "Over there in that small garden; it's my favorite spot. Let's sit over there." The priest looks over at a black cast iron bench under the lamppost. "The lights blown." She pulls him by his hand, "Come on." "Well Okay, not so fast." She sits down and speaks, "Sit here." The priest sits down beside her. The creature climbs into the tree behind them. She places her head on his shoulder, looks out the corner of her eyes, and sees the red eyes of the creature. The priest feels eerie, "I feel a cold chill." She expresses, "You know how the night can get here in L.A." "Well, how much further do we have?" She gives him a devious look, "This is it." The priest, surprised, "Right here, outside?" She leans close to his face and strongly whispers, "No one can see us."

The priest's nervous, "You're kidding, right? It's chilly out here." She smirks and begins to slide down onto her knees, "I have something to warm you up." He tries to lift her, "You can't, hey." "Shh." she hushes him, unzips the crotch of his zipper, and gives oral pleasure. She looks up at him as he reaches his point; she sees the demons red eyes grow big in anticipation. She knows it's time. As he ejaculates, she continues.

Suddenly, the priest yells, "Yowl!" and grabs her hair and pulls. She yanks him down and jams her black leather gloves into his mouth. A slurping sound overwhelms his groans as he pulls frantically to lift her. She raves like a mad bulldog, and sucks three pints of blood from his crotch. As she lifts, the tortured priest spits out the leather gloves and yells, "you crazy whore; you bit me!" Connie stands up and wipes her mouth, with an evil face, "Serves you right you sick bastard, how dare you take advantage of us helpless little women." The priest, in shock, pulls up his pants as he yells, "Call 911!" He tries to grab her, as she steps back and laughs, "You sorry little dick, nobody hears you; Go home to mommy." The priest's, bent over in pain, looks around to see if any businesses are open. He begins to stagger off, while groaning as he holds himself. Connie laughs, "That's right reverend, go home to mommy and confess of what a bad boy you've been tonight; Tell her a whore bit your cock!" The priest runs for help.

The shaking tree interrupts Connie, as she turns, "Bam!" she's knocked down on her side and is mounted by the demon. It growls at her and slashes her face with its claw as it jumps off her. The priest runs to a clothing store, but the door is locked. The front of his pant's soaked in blood. He begins to panic and cry out, "Somebody help me, call 911, please!"

He tries each door, but is startled by the sound of a growl. The priest realizes that something is in the dark, but he's not able to see it. He begins to run to the street corner and locates a coffee shop; it's closed, but there's a payphone. The priest quickly limps toward the payphone, which lies five hundred feet away. With lost of breath, he grows faint and his vision blurs. As he gets one hundred feet from his point, his mouth begins to foam. The rapid movement of the priest causes his heart to pump the vampires' virus through his veins. The burning sensation of his throat makes him fall down and grab his neck. As he rolls, and begins to get up from his back, he sees the eyes of the demon.

The priest screams, "Help, ah!" The demon jumps on top of him and roars into his face, revealing its fangs. The demon slashes the priest face and stretches his mouth open. As the priest yells, the demon begins to glow as a flash of lightning enters into the priest.

Eight o'clock rolls around and Roy thinks to himself of how hungry he should feel. Instead of hunger, he's thirsty, grabs a glass, and fills it with tap water. Before he drinks, the smell of worms from the glass makes him nauseous. With the thought of being sick again, he pours the water back. Remembering the water from Womack, he turns and briskly walks to his closet and slips on another pair of boots. Roy walks out to his factory brown nineteen seventy nine classic Chevrolet Corvette Stingray. Opening the door, he sits, and breaks the seat and bends the axle. Slowly getting up, he shuts the door and starts towards the local corner store. While walking, he notices his change of attitude, and how things just don't get to him like it used to. A smile comes over his face as he speaks, "I should have been mad about my car."

At the store, he buys a twelve pack of purified water, goes out the door, pulls a bottle of water out of his bag and begins to drink. He walks a half block, where stands the Foxes Tail Lounge. This is the weekend hot spot where many upper class and famous celebrity's party. Roy crosses the street; he doesn't want to go past the line of anxious clubbers waiting to get in. When he gets across, he notices red eyes, which flashes between two buildings in the alley. He stops and hides behind the parking meter and car. Roy smells a stink like sulfur and electrical wires burning; the demons prowl the wall of the building. Their eyes look towards the club. Two men nicely dressed in suits meet a woman who steps out of a limousine. She's dressed in black leather and crosses the street with the men. They head between the two buildings towards the demons. The men begin to fondle her.

Roy hears it, the noise, it's the sound of the demons speaking to each other as they stand on the wall, and watch the woman and two men make out. Roy's curious and begins to inch over to the corner of the building to take a glance. As his head looks around, he spots the two tall muscular men, one in front and the other behind her. The woman begins to nibble the ear of the guy facing her. The demons make a growling noise in excitement, as they await the vampiress to strike again.

Roy's attention focuses from the woman to the demons. Roy has the feeling that a person gets when they hold a new nine-volt battery against their tongue. The feeling of energy causes the hairs on his body to rise. As he looks up, his eyes glow blue. The demons see him and yell out "Ah!" as they fly away.

The woman hears the demons and turns, causing the men to be startled. They look, where Roy stands with a bag in his arms. The closest man yells out, "You got a problem boy?" They both stop their action and start towards him. She yells out, "Hold on." The two men stop and allow her between them. It's Connie; she stands facing Roy. She's able to see the blue from his eyes. She glances at his feet and then upward and speaks, "I'll meet you in the club boys." The taller guy looks at her, "Are you sure?" "Yes, I'll be just fine." They give Roy a bad look, as they walk by. She has the impression that he's a werewolf, because of the reflection of his eyes; she approaches him. "Come here." Roy just stands and stares at her. He knows that something is different about her. He smells the fresh blood of another person on her. Her eyes are dark black. "Did you hear me, come here and kneel down." She opens her mouth and hisses, revealing her sharp fangs. A rumbling sound emits from her voice as she commands, "Don't you know who I am, kneel dog!" She gets close to him and pulls back her hand to slap, "Swish." she misses his face. Roy, unaware of his lightning speed, realizes that he surprised her by moving his face back. Connie stops in her track, and is astonished that a werewolf would disobey her orders and could dodge her quickness. He smiles and then gives her an angry look as he turns and walks off into the night.

*

The Foxes Hole

Out of a black limousine steps the owner of the Foxes Tail Lounge. He's a five foot eleven blonde hair Albino with dark grey eyes. The chauffeur opens the door as the owner walks on red carpet leading to the front entrance. Inside the club lays a stage and small casino bar with dance floor, and an eloquent diner which seats two hundred guest. There's rumor of a one story underground private designer clothing store called the Foxes Hole, where only the wealthy are allowed to shop. This underground store is said to house twelve elaborate suites rented for one hundred thousand dollars a weekend and two hundred and fifty thousand a week.

The owners elite staff is all hand selected; Out of the two hundred and fifty employees, one hundred and twenty are vampires, a mixture of male and female bodyguards. These are the owners' personal caretakers of the affairs of the club. Sitting inside at the owners' private booth is the two men dressed in top dollar suits. The owner joins them for wine "Gentlemen, may I pose a toast to your new partnership with the Lounge." Connie walks in and joins them. She speaks softly, "Sorry for the little mix up fellows." The taller man speaks, "We thought we lost you there for a moment." Connie insists, "Oh, that guy out there, he was a friend that I knew from high school. He was just making arrangements for an alumni party here at the Lounge." The owner looks in curiosity, "Oh really now?" Connie replies, "Yeah, don't you remember from last week?" The owner catches on to her plot to cover her incident. "Oh yes, now that you mention it, I do remember now." The two men nod their heads and smile. The owner smiles back and speaks, "Gentlemen, I believe Connie has some wonderful things to show you." The taller man lustfully glances at Connie and speaks, "Most definitely wonderful." The owner stands, "After you gentlemen." They stand and walk towards the private back entrance where awaits two large bodyguards in front of a large seven inch door made of solid Gold. The taller man's in amaze, "Hey, is this gold?" Connie sensually replies, "Of course it is."

The shorter man looks over the door where there's writing and inquires, "What does that say?" The owner replies, "It reads The Foxes Hole. It's written in ancient Greek. That inscription is more than two thousand years old. Our anthropologist uncovered and replenished its original luster." The short man eyes grow big, "Wow, that's an awesome discovery. It fit's the place well." The owner stops as the guards open the door. The tall man wonders, "Aren't you going with us?" "Oh no, I have a meeting to attend, I will join you for dinner later tonight; Connie will be your guide." They smile and shake hands.

As the men begin into the entrance, the owner leans towards Connie's ear and strongly whispers, "What happened?" "One of your puppies didn't obey my orders. I warned you that owning too many of them could lead to trouble. He just stood there looking as if he was going to eat me up." "Well, which one was it?" "Hell, I don't know, it was one of your new one's, the bald black guy around my height, he wears black boots." The owners face goes blank; he doesn't recall any of his werewolves fitting that description.

Connie goes through the door, turns, and puckers her lips at him, "Bye now." She smirks as the door closes. Down the red carpet hall, lays an elevator; Connie and the men enter and go down to the Foxes Hole. The taller of the men is Dan Gordon, one of the wealthiest men in Southern California. The other is Kyle Theodore Hutchinson, a well-known CEO of British United Airways and the Boeing Hutchinson Corporation; He is cited as being one of the top twelve wealthiest men in the world. Connie shows them the illustrious department store, which sells some of the most exquisite furs in the world. Facing the store is the Foxes Winery, where is told that the Queen of England bought a bottle of wine for a half million dollars.

Connie flirts, "Boy's before I show you the rest, lest take a look at where you will be staying for the evening." She unlocks a beautiful suite, which houses a one hundred foot aquarium. As they enter, the men begin to kiss her. "Now, the bed room suite." She falls back onto the custom king size bed. Removing her fur, the men undress for sexual eroticism.

The lights are dim; Connie mounts Hutchinson while Gordon pleasures her from behind. Connie begins to tongue kiss Hutchinson, as sounds of moans echoes through the room.

Hutchinson reaches his orgasm; Connie kisses his neck, which slowly turns into nibbles of passion. She suddenly bites him and places her hands over his mouth. He tries to move but she's too strong, as his muffled scream turns into a low groan. Gordon, unaware of his partners' state, begins to reach his point in arousal, while Connie turns, giving him oral pleasure. She swallows, As Gordon smiles and looks down at his partner, "Damn, this dame is the best, huh Kyle?" Kyle lays dormant. Gordon looks over Connie's shoulder while shaking Hutchinson's leg. "You didn't pass out from all the excitement did you?" Gordon looks again and sees the blood on his neck. His eyes widen as he hollers, "What happened?" "Thump!" Connie jumps on Gordon's neck, causing him to fall onto his back. He screams out as she raves on his juggler. He scratches and pulls at her hair, but is not able to break the arms around his neck. With his feet kicking, his eyes roll back as his mouth opens without making sound. The mad slurping sound is herd as Connie holds tight; her jujitsu chokehold soon turns a squirming muscle man into a motionless corpse. Loudly moaning, she gives herself sexual pleasure. Connie stands and walks to the stove, where brazes a brander over a burning stovetop. She walks into the room and presses the hot sear; the smoke from the brand lifts as she marks the necks of the new vampires.

Roy returns to his apartment. The first thing he wants to do is get some sleep, but the only problem is that he's not sleepy. His bed slams into the floor as it crumbles at his weight. "Shit, what the hell is going on?" He sits on the floor and thinks back to the time he experienced his battle with the angelic creature. Puzzled, he rushes into his study room and turns on the computer. He searches the internet in hopes to find clues on his experience. After extensive study and research, he looks at the time on the computer. He speaks out, "Oh shit, it's eight in the morning; I guess I stayed up all night." He reaches over and answers the phone before it rings. He speaks, "Yeah?" "Mr. Johnson, This is your Broker Mr. Simms, and I was just reminding you of our appointment at ten." "Yeah, I have it down on my calendar and I'll be there in the morning."

Mr. Simms comments, "Um, tomorrow, but I thought you wanted to meet today?" Roy laughs, "Man, I didn't know the bank opened on Sundays." Mr. Simms is dumbfounded, "Sunday? Mr. Johnson, today's Monday." His voice squeaks, "You're joking, it's not Monday, it's Sunday." "No Mr. Johnson I'm not joking, it's really Monday. You must have gotten your days mixed up or something." Roy's heart jumps, as he turns and looks at his calendar on the wall. "Wait a minute, hold on." "Okay." replies Mr. Simms.

With his mouth hanging open, Roy walks back to his computer and clicks on the date. A shock goes through his body as he realizes that two nights have gone by. "Fuck!" "Are you Okay?" remarks Mr. Simms. "Yeah, yeah, I'm alright. Damn, I'll be there at nine forty five." "Okay, I'll see you then." Roy, with a scratchy sound, speaks, "Okay, see you later." The phone hangs up. The thought baffles him as he realizes that time seemed to go by extremely fast. He never got tired or even yawned once. The problem is that he was out of water and was thirsty. Roy bathes from the sink and throws on fresh jeans and a dress shirt. He goes to his closet for his favorite last pair of boots. He looks at his other pairs, and sees that they are completely busted. He decides to wear his last pair of boots at the bank. Roy calls the same cab service that he used at the airport, and makes his way to meet his banker for the loan.

The cab arrives. Roy opens the door and slowly gets in. His weight is supported normally. He scratches his head as he tells the driver his destination. In the taxi, the taxi driver looks down at Roy's feet. He holds his boots on his lap and notices, "Oh, I've been wearing these boots all weekend and my feet are sore. I just want to put them on when I go into the bank." The taxi driver nods, "I can understand that buddy, that's why I wear these tennis shoes. You should buy some; they're really comfortable." Roy glances over and makes up a story, "Yeah, I was just going to buy some new shoes today. Where did you get those?" "I got these at the little shoe store on the corner of Hollywood Boulevard and Wilton." Roy smiles, "Thanks, I'll go there and check em out." "They cost me a couple hundred of bucks, but they're worth every penny. Take my word for it; you'll see."

They arrive. "Hey, I'll pay you five hundred dollars if you hang around until I'm done in the bank." "Are you serious?" Roy hands him two hundred dollars. "I'll pay you the rest if you hang around."

The taxi driver's ecstatic, "Hell yeah, take your time." Roy puts on his shoes and walks into the bank. After an hour and a half, Roy returns to the taxi. "I thought you'd be gone by now." he hands the man three hundred bucks. A look of shock goes over the taxi drivers' face as he lets out a chuckle, "So, where to now, home?" "Naw, I'd like to go to a friend I know, he has a shop six miles from here on Crenshaw Boulevard." The cab driver looks over, "Sure, I can do that." The taxi drives away. They pull up to the shop. Roy holds his boots as he steps out of the taxi. He goes into the front entrance of the steel shop, owned by James Blacksmith. Blacksmith's been a friend of the Johnson's since Roy was a little baby in Knoxville Tennessee. He's known for his fine work in making titanium steel art and furniture, which are displayed in various museums and exhibits around the nation. After the war, Blacksmith settled in Los Angeles, where he ran into Roy at a festival in Santa Monica.

The cowbells on the door jingle as Roy walks into the storefront. A Grey haired dark skinned black man turns and lets out a happy shout, "Damn man, look what the cats dragged in; They let you out of the hell hole?" He goes around the display case and gives Roy a big hug. Blacksmith smiles, "Whatcha been into; How you doing?" "Oh, I'm out for a while." "Really, well I bet you're happy about that." He scopes Roy over, "Man, you're looking good." Roy nods and responds, "Yep." "So, how's your mom and dad doing?" "Oh, they're doing great." Blacksmith grins, "How long are you in for?" "I'm in for a few months." Blacksmith smiles and nods his head, "Man, I know you needed that."

After fifteen minutes of great-shared memories, he notices Roy in his socks. He joyfully looks, "What happened to your shoes?" Roy hustles an answer, "Oh, I busted these on a parachute jump. I want to know if you can fix my soles." He looks the boots over, "Damn, it looks like an elephant stepped on your foot." Blacksmith remembers the same sight when a large boulder at a mineshaft crushed a man's steel-toed boots. "Hey, I got a job for you when you get a chance. Could you make me some furniture?" "What do you mean can I make you some furniture? You know I can make anything." Roy grins, "Well, it just might be anything, cause by the time I'm done, you might not want to make anymore furniture." They both laugh. He looks down at his boots and remembers the steel shoes Blacksmith once made at a museum.

Roy picks them up and speaks, "These are the same boots my momma got me when I first went into service. Well, I'd like to have all of it made out of steel, except the leather part." "You want the toes made out of steel too?" "Yeah, and make em good, cause I might show them off to some of my friends." Blacksmith picks one up, "If you wear these boots, they'll be so heavy that you won't be able to walk." "That's alright though, its fun and games anyway." Blacksmith found it odd that Roy wants his heels made out of titanium steel. He thought Roy would make a display out of them, but was certain to make them comfortable enough to wear just in case he wears them to a party, besides it would be a great way to display some of his artwork.

After three hours, Blacksmith hands Roy the finished boots. He gets down on one knee and pulls the boots on. He arranges for Blacksmith to come over with his equipment and custom make reinforced furniture. Blacksmith laughs. Roy walks out, "I'll leave the extra key for you just in case I'm not in." "Okay man, I'll see you tomorrow." Roy's happy; a new pair of boots is born. He returns to his apartment, calls Mrs. Randall, and arranges to meet her Tuesday morning. She's very happy to hear that he came up with the money. Roy celebrates his new soon to be ownership of the illustrious castle apartment as he downs three bottled waters. When the day darkens, his mind begins to wander as he thinks of all the mishaps, which has befallen him since the dawn of eve. His logic is defined, a much unusual thought pattern than what he's used to; His sense of touch with humanity soon fades.

Roy looks at the empty bottles, "I've got to get some more water." He makes his way back towards the local grocery. Across the street from the Foxes Lounge is a newsstand. Roy reaches into his pocket for change to buy a newspaper. The front-page article catches his eye, "Troops Lost in Terrorist Attack in Egypt." As he lifts the paper out of the bin, something else catches his eye.

Roy notices the crates outside the Lounge. They have military markings from Womack. He realizes that these are the same crates used to give blood transfusions to military hospitals across the United States. "What the hell is blood supplies doing over there." He watches as the men use the forklift and dollies to transport the packages into the Lounge.

Roy gets closer to watch, but a bodyguard stops him and speaks, "Hey bud, you can't go in this way, you have to go in the front." Roy begins to walk away and responds, "Oh Okay, thanks." Trouble awaits, but Roy knows that there's reason behind all madness; the only thing, is the logic of the madness. His curiosity sends him on a mission to work his way into the Foxes Tail Lounge. He paces towards the front entrance with a brisk walk of a man who would be going places in big business. Roy knows that it's acting time, and he must put on his best performance. The night is young as a hound dog is on the loose and smells blood, a foxes blood.

＊

Gargoyle versus Vampires

Roy approaches under the red canopy leading to the entrance of the Foxes Tail Lounge. Walking past the valet parking guides and the body-guard, he opens the door where the host and three seating assistants stand. "Yes, may I have your name sir?" "Roy Johnson." The host looks up his name, "Sir, I'm sorry, but your name's not coming up. Did you make reservations?" "No, I was just walking by, and I saw your nice building and thought I'd check it out. I'd like to try out your menu." "Well, we are so sorry Mr. Johnson, but our seats are reservation only." "Well okay, then I'd like to reserve a table."

The host looks serious, "Mr. Johnson, are you aware of our fees here?" "Sure I am." "How many in your party?" "Just one, I'm alone." "Sir, that would be twenty five thousand dollars." In shock, Roy speaks, "For how many people?" "Sir that's twenty five thousand a person." With a disgusted look, Roy reluctantly answers, "Sure, go ahead and charge me." The host search records in the computer, "Sir, I am sorry, but it appears that you are not a member. Are you aware of our membership here?" "Are you kidding me; What for?" "Well, that's just policy here at the lounge, you must have a membership." "Why?" "Well, this is a private club and the membership's a hundred thousand each, for six months. In order to join, you must contract for five years." "How do I contract?" "You have to set up an appointment with the manager or his assistant, and when your application is accepted, and then you'd get a membership."

A tall large bodyguard approaches, "Excuse me, but we are going to have to ask you to leave, I'm sorry for the misunderstanding, but this is a private club." Roy knows that his actions are important and begins, "You guys have no idea who you're dealing with; I could be working with your owner." Another guard joins the bodyguard, as they begin to walk Roy out. He thinks quickly, "I thought I was supposed to get a free meal." The guard looks with disbelief, "How do you figure?" He hustles, "I work for Womack." the guard looks at the other guard and turns to Roy, "You one of the delivery guys?" He shakes his head, "Yeah. We just got done with a run tonight." "Let me see your I.D."

Roy pulls out his military I.D. and hands it over." The guard carefully looks it over and hands it back. "Oh, I'm sorry about that; Dinner starts at eight. Our host will take you to the wardrobe for your fitting. As you know the policy here, all employees and affiliates must wear the proper attire."

Seven thirty evening, Roy's fitted into a black tuxedo in the men's bathroom, which houses two showers and a dressing room. At eight, he's seated alone in the employees section. A waitress approaches, "Sir, may we start you out with some appetizers?" "Sure, I'll have the soup and spinach dip with tortillas." "And for your drink?" "I'll just have water." "Thank you Mr. Johnson, I'll be back with your water." She turns to walk away and is halted, "Wait a second, do you have bottled water?" "Yes sir, we do have bottled water." "Is it that mountain kind or the purified?" "It's purified." "Good, then I'll take two of those." "Okay, that's two bottled waters, vegetable soup and spinach dip; I'll be right back." While waiting, Roy gets up and walks around. As he strolls through the eloquent restaurant, the murals and paintings on the ceiling and walls impress him. He approaches an entrance, which leads to the casino and dance lounge.

Roy's clothing cloaks his identity as he passes the two bodyguards. The casino overflows with classy guest. The workers are topless; the men wear black slacks and bow ties and the women wear pink bow ties with black slacks laced in pink. The waitress returns to Roy's empty seat; she looks around to see if he went to the restroom. One of the bodyguards notices her unusual behavior and steps forward to ask, "What are you looking for?" "My guest, I lost my guest. Did you see a bald guy come through here?" "No." She shakes her head, "Oh well, he'll be back." The guard radios the head bodyguard, "Kendall, what's the story on table six?"

Kendall Drarcinelli's in charge when Connie's not around. He responds, "What the hell are you talking about, table six? There's no employee guest on our list for tonight; who arranged the seating?" He responds nervously, "It was Bruce, he scheduled for the Womack guys." A fiery look hits Kendall's eyes as he speaks, "I'll be down there." Kendall walks towards table six and is approached by Bruce. "Hey, I thought the Womack guys were eating tonight." Kendall answers, "No, they're not." Bruce hastily, "Well, he's in the casino right now; what do you want me to do?"

Kendall walks to the casino's entrance. He looks at Roy's eyes and speaks, "This one's canine; Must be the one Connie was talking about. Get Sarah to show him around; Sarah's the top host in the casino." Sarah prances towards Roy, "Hello Mr. Johnson, I'm Sarah, your host here at Foxes Casino. Would you like for me to show you around?" "No thanks, I've seen the place." Her eyes glimmer, "Oh, so you've seen our stores?" "Your stores; Where at?" "Well, its underground, would you like for me to give you a tour?" "Sure." Roy walks behind the topless attractive host; He knows she's a vampire. She leads Roy through to the gold door. There are no bodyguards there. She reaches for her belt buckle and detaches a large gold key shaped like a fox's tail. As she unlocks the door, she looks up and explains, "This is called the Foxes Hole." She looks at him and flashes, "You like my key?" Roy smiles, "Its funny looking." "Well, it's my belt buckle. They give all the head host one; it's sexy like a fox, don't you think?" As she dangles the key near his face, he takes a closer look and responds, "Well, I guess it's kind of sexy." The door makes a loud clicking sound as it shuts behind Roy and Sarah. He speaks up, "Man, that's a solid door." Sarah glances back, "Oh yeah, it's made out of over seven inches of solid gold; Pretty cool huh?" Roy eyebrows down, "Damn, that's a lot of money." Sarah raises her eyebrows, "Well, I really don't know what it cost, but I was told by the staff that it's worth over a billion." Roy with enthusiasm, "I'll say it cost that and more." As they approach the elevator, Roy anticipates, "Hey Sarah, um, I'm kind of nervous on elevators; Well, I just can't ride on them for personal reasons, is there some stairs we could go down instead?" "I guess, I mean, what ever makes our guest happy." They walk pass the elevators to a brass door which leads to a stairwell. She uses her key to open the door as they walk down the spiral stairs." Roy's amazed of the beauty of the stairs, "Is this gold too?" "No, this is brass railing." At the bottom of the stair is another door, which leads into a foyer. Four bodyguards walk in the other direction as Sarah turns and looks deeply into Roy's eyes, she begins to speak, but shakes it off as she unlocks the door. Roy excites, "Wow, this is cool." Sarah smiles, "I told you so." She escorts Roy to the clothing store. A store clerk greets him, "Welcome Mr. Johnson, may I assist you on your purchase tonight?"

Roy looks into the seam of a coat and notices the pricing, over fifty thousand dollars, "No, I'm just looking tonight." The clerk smiles, "Well, with all pleasure, let us know if we could assist you in anyway." "Thanks, I will." Roy gazes through the aisles. After looking at what he thought was the most ridiculous prices, he lets out a hard breath and speaks, "Well, I guess I'm done here Sarah." "Okay then Mr. Johnson, follow me; I'm sure you will like our suites." "You have hotels down here?" "Yes, and we have a wonderful winery too." Maybe we can get you some complimentary wine and cheese on our way back up." She leads Roy into a large suite, where sets a fireplace and ivory grand piano. "Wow, this is really nice, and I like the big screen television; it makes it look like your outside." Sarah smiles, "Yes, that's a giant screen saver. It's showing a full moon and twinkling stars, romantic huh?" She struts into the bedroom and calls, "Look at this grand master bed, it's in the shape of a harp. It actually plays music when you lay on it."

Sarah spreads out on the bed, "Oh, I could use a break right now." She looks up, but Roy's still in the living room looking at the piano. She stands and slowly walks in. He sits down and presses a key. She speaks up, "That's sexy too, isn't it?" "Sure it is. I like pianos; this one's real nice." She prances over toward Roy and eases down beside him. Her pretty blue eyes flutter, "I sure could use a break right about now." Roy turns his head and looks deeply into her eyes. It suddenly dawns on her that he never looked at her breast, just her face.

Staring at Roy, Sarah's bright blue eyes begin to tear up. "You're a nice guy; I can tell that there's not one bad bone in you." He squints, "What made you say that?" "It's the way you look at me; Well, I..." Roy interrupts, "I know you're different, you're not like normal girls." Sarah's surprised and jitter's, "What are you talking about?" He looks steadfast, "I don't believe in vampires, they don't exist." Sarah leans back in shock, "I'm sorry." Roy's eyes begin to glisten, "I know you are my decoy." Sarah breathes heavy as a tear falls, "In just the little time I've met you, there's something so attractive about you. I really like you; I don't want to hurt you." She rises up, "I'm Sorry Roy." He stands and walks to her, "So where's your fangs?" Tears fall, as she utters, "I don't have fangs."

Roy leans close as his breath hits her face, "So, how many people have you've killed?" She grabs for his neck, "Bam!" she's knocked on the floor as Roy holds both her arms and places his eyes close to hers, "You smell like someone else's blood." She cries, "I've never killed a person in my life!" She tries to pull her hands loose but is unsuccessful. As she looks into his eyes, she realizes that his eyes are unlike the color of any werewolf she's seen. Sarah hisses as she tries to shake loose, "What are you?" Roy smiles and lets go of her arms as he stands. "You'd better get out of here; it's going to get ugly."

While rubbing her bruised arm, Sarah sits up and rises onto her feet. "This is the first time I've ever confronted a canine, but then again, you're no wolf are you?" Roy hears the heart beat of ten vampires as he turns and speaks, "They're outside." Sarah gives him the look of regret and walks out. As she goes out, she looks at Kendall, "He knows you're here." Kendall and Bruce walk in with eight bodyguards. He commands, "Come here dog; Kneel." Roy smirks without a word. Perturbed, he speaks, "You mother fucking piece of shit, when I say bark, you bark and when I say kneel, you kneel, bitch!" Roy speaks, "Oh, so you must be Kendall and you're Bruce and you're Mike, Jesse, Tom, Bobby, Clyde, Jerrod, Van and Damon; what a fucked up bunch of freaks."

Bruce, surprised, "How the hell do you know us?" Roy blinks, "I have good ears. Besides, your closed channel radios aren't so private." Kendall reacts, "Everybody knows that canines have excellent hearing. Too bad no one's going to hear you." Jerrod and Damon place the silencers on their Tech Nines. Kendall figures it would be hard to stop him as a werewolf. He speaks, "Shoot this bitch if he starts to change into a dog."

Roy knows their vampires and is aware of the weapons underneath their clothes. He waits as his ears tune in to the blood pumping through their veins. "I know what, you're going to tell me that I should not have been snooping around and you're going to teach me a valuable lesson, right?" Kendall reacts, "No, that's not it at all; you see, you're a canine and you know the pack between us, but there's one problem, you don't obey the pack; and that's just not right. Since when did your kind start acting on your own? That's a big no-no when it comes to our relationship. When daddy comes home, he's going to be pissed to know that one of his little puppies' gone mad, so, it's time to put Old Yellow to sleep."

Roy catches on, "So, I'm supposed to be your pound puppy? Well that's a messed up family, cause I don't like the dog-food masters been bringing to the table; it's not cooked. And you know what happens when a dog gets the taste of blood." Bruce swings, "Swish!" Roy fakes back as his foot cracks Bruce's chin open. "Plop!" he hit's the floor with a broken jaw. Mike pulls out a switchblade as Jesse tries to grab Roy; a snapping sound of Mikes arm sends the blade flying across the room. Before Jesse grips Roy, he sores backward, crashing into the piano. Tom, Clyde, Bobby, and Van frantically attacks, but are not able to touch him. Van looks back at Kendall, "I thought you said this mother fucker was a canine." "He is." "Well, he's too damned fast!" Roy continues to dodge their punches. Clyde flies into the air in hopes of landing on top of Roy. "Kaboom!" the hard tile floor halts Clyde face down. "Pop!" Bobby's leg is knocked out of socket by the foot of the swift evader. "Swoosh!" Van plunges up side down into the bathroom shower, blood flows out of his mouth.

Kendall is the largest and strongest of the bodyguards. He realizes that Roy's faster than any of the wolves he's fought in the past. Roy turns and faces Kendall who stands in front of Jerrod and Damon, who's ready to shoot him. As Kendall approaches, Roy dropkicks his groin, "Clump!" Kendall drops to his knees. Suddenly, the sound of silenced tech nines unloads, as it feels like small gnats hitting Roy's chest. Snapping into the reality of being shot, Roy looks for the door and darts, "flashoop!" he disappears from their sight. Stopping at the lower level brass door, he realizes he got past them. "There he is!" The sound of guns rage through the hall as he pulls at the door. "Bam!" a flash goes as he finds himself in the hallway leading to the casino. Two body guards recognize him and pulls out nine millimeters, "Bang, bang bang!" another flash of light, and

Roy's standing outside. Kendall runs up and searches, "Where the hell did he go?" "Out there!" yells a host as she notices Roy standing under the canopy. Before Kendall's able to get out, Roy hears them and runs down the street. At his apartment, he comes to grips to the craziness of the action he witnessed. "Damn, I know I got shot." He looks at his suit filled with bullet holes, rushes to the mirror and pulls it off, revealing an unharmed body. The thought of how he got out so fast, without realizing it, baffles him as he gazes at his torso.

The reality settles in; the Gargoyle accepts his fate. There's more to him than meets the eye. He knows he has to get to the root of how he became a new creation. Roy thinks of how he would go back to Egypt; he hopes to find some evidence of his new awakening experience. A question lurks, "Who am I?"

❈

The Burning Quest

The sun rises as glistering beams hit the eyes of an already alert body lying on the hard floor. Roy stands up, walks to the window, and watches the beauty of the fire in the sky, peaking through the white puffy clouds. The world seen shadows the unseen world; His new-found eyes catches two six-inch shiny snow-white flute shaped creatures being chased by black birds. Being able to hear everything and see everything is not easy for him. This magical moment seems like a fairy tale, but it's not a dream; it's real.

The buzzard sounds; it's Blacksmith. Roy answers the intercom, "Come on up man." Blacksmith and two of his crewmembers holding tape measures and rulers ascend the stairs. The doors open, "Come on in." Blacksmith in cheer, "Hey man, this is nice." Roy smiles, "Well, you see all this stuff in here, you can have it." Blacksmith grins, "Are you sure?" "Yeah, I want all this stuff out, the bed the sofa, everything." Blacksmith answers, "I brought my truck." He points, "This is Matt and Tevon; they work with me." Roy shakes their hands.

Roy guides Blacksmith through his apartment and describes how he wants it remodeled. He leaves Blacksmith a check for twenty thousand dollars. Getting into the cab, he makes way to meet Mrs. Randall. After a couple of hours of transactions, the taxi driver awaits, as the new owner comes out of the bank, smiling and giving a grey-headed woman a hug. Tears flow from her eyes, "I know it's in good hands." "Yes maam," Roy pats her hand and kisses her cheek. "You are welcomed anytime Mrs. Randall. Her eyes light up, "Well, I just might drop in on you sometime." Roy smiles, "Sure, I would like that." He gets into the cab and waves, "See you later." The cab heads to the market; He stocks up on ten cases of bottled water.

During the six days of his new ownership, Roy stays in the empty apartment below, while a toiling Blacksmith molds a new abode for the gargoyle. He's set up shop, a lap top and desktop computer sets on the old desk. Beneath the grinding sounds of steal, being buffed to perfection, Roy answers the phone, "Hello?" A woman answers, "Hello, hello, is this the Kings Palace Apartments?" "Yes it is."

The woman in surprise, "Get out of here! I didn't finish dialing the last number, and the phone just picks up. Now that's kinky." Roy interrupts, "How may I help you?" "Oh, I'm sorry darling, I was responding to your ad, and I wanted to know if you still had the two bedroom, bath and a half with den and fireplace available?" "Yes, it is still available." "Really, are you serious?" "Yes." "Great! Is it still thirty two hundred a month?" "Yes, it is." Ecstatic, she cheers, "Awesome! I want to rent that one." "Well, first I need to check your credit and schedule you for an interview. How about tomorrow?" "Tomorrow's fine." "And, what's your name?" "Oh, I'm sorry darling, this is Kelly Starrlight." Roy's mouth drops, "Are you talking, The-Kelly-Starrlight? The one from the soap opera and who just made the blockbuster hit, Never Bend a Buck?" Tickled, "Yes, that's me." Enthused, Roy replies, "I thought I recognized your voice; I know that voice from anywhere. I used to watch you on the morning show everyday. I saw Never Bend a Buck three times; Congratulations on winning four Oscars." "Well, thank you darling."

Roy's curious, "So, out of all the places in the world, what made you want to rent here? I mean, you are the highest paid actress in the world, surely you could buy any place in Los Angeles or Hollywood for all that matters." "Well, my agent spotted your ad, and I looked it over and I really like your set up, the security and privacy lot, the pool and hot tub is awesome. We actually did some research on the place, which dates back in the early eighteen hundreds. This was owned by the royal family for generations, so when I saw it, I just fell in love with it." Roy knows it's really her; He's followed her since he was a teenager when she first became a super model. Besides being the greatest female actress, Kelly is well known for her exotic body and intoxicating eyes. Roy speaks, "Well, since I know all about you, I know I won't have to run a credit check on you. It would be my honor to meet you." Kelly interrupts, "Oh dear sweet, I am filming in New York right now; is it okay for my agent to come by and pick up the lease?" "Sure, how about nine thirty?" "That sounds fine." Roy jots the time down in his planner, "So, at nine thirty, I will be expecting…?" "Oh, his name is Jamie O'Conner." Roy speaks, "I know who that is; He helped produce your last film." "That's right, and he's still the top agent for Time Warner."

Roy smiles, "Great. I look forward to having you as our new resident." She giggles, "Okay sugar pop, see you later, bye bye." He hangs up.

Roy has spent the last six days and nights reading and studying religions and ancient myth; nothing makes sense as too many doctrines cloud his logic, leaving him distastefulness for any denomination. He concludes that no one religion is right, that they all lack the fullness of anything relevant to history and time; There's no solid evidence of mans creation or the origin of angels. He remembers the many years his mother sent him to Sunday school and the readings of the King James Bible and how he foolishly believed in something he could not see or explain; But now, he's sure that everything he believed is but a story told by common men. His desire to find the truth turns his religious beliefs into questions of reason. Looking into the mirror, he realizes that the world's religions are only a mere blanket, which covers the truth. There is a world hidden from the eyes of men, wondered by the minds of believers and told by the mouths of silence. He aspirates air out of his nose and speaks to the mirror, "What am I?"

It's Tuesday morning, the birds chirp and the smell of black java emits through the window; Prevailing without a yawn or fatigue, steady bright amber eyes reads the history of the Dead Sea scrolls. Roy's aware that the internet is full of every kind of twisted information a man could attain, but still, he grudgingly seeks answers to the missing puzzle of his wake. "Wfff." He takes a breath and looks up over his computer screen;

it's the smell of fresh brewed coffee and bran muffins. Roy's sure he can taste them. "What the hell?" His eyes snaps out of the daze; "The coffee shop is a half mile away." He jumps up from his chair and rushes to the opened window, closes his eyes and presses his nose against the screen and sniffs. The humming sounds vibrate his ears as he opens his eyes to a new world. Tiny microscopic creatures moving in every direction whistles by, as the new spectator is spellbound.

A child plays outside on his tricycle; the laughter gives Roy an adrenaline rush, as his heart jumps in his chest. It's the same feeling he got when he was a child who found new toys waiting under the Christmas tree. A woman listening to her walkman jogs by, Roy hears the music as if he was wearing the headphones. He picks up the emotions from her face as his heart begins to pound harder. No, it's not her looks, but her overwhelming facial expressions; He knows she's running off her stress.

The Hispanic man across the street has a leaf blower and begins to curse at the wind for blowing his leaves in the opposite direction. Roy smirks. The wind blows again as a voice whispers, "Shit." Roy anticipated the word; he knew what the man would say before he spoke. Roy breathes heavy; It is as if he could feel the emotions himself, but yet, it was far greater; Something he's never felt before. It's better than the bottled water, it's better than food; it's a pleasure, which sends energy through his body, his hunger is filled.

This newfound knowledge brings Roy into the realization that he's been living off the emotionalism of every living thing that crosses his path. The smells and sights as well as the knowledge gathered from all his research has been the very thing, which kept him fed. He begins to think of the old saying that knowledge is power and brings it into a realization that some how and some way, it is food for his wellbeing.

The energy of confidence and joy emits from a man who drives up in a dark blue Mercedes with tinted windows. Roy's newfound sight is able to see through the tint; He knows it's Time Warner agent, Jamie O'Conner. Just as he begins to press the button, the large golden-white gate opens. A voice is heard, "Hello Mr. O'Conner, there's parking in the rear." O'Conner's impressed, "Is this Mr. Johnson?" "Yes sir, I have the contract, I'm in apartment one." "Okay, I'll be around." He parks and walks to the front of the complex. He loves the two white lion statues facing the walkway. The door has a large brass lion head knocker with a button at its snout. Before he presses the buzzard, a click is heard as the magnet releases, allowing him to walk in. Inside, is a large white oak and brass stairwell, surrounded by a marble and stone foyer. There are paintings of lions, knights and dragons in battle.

To the left center is a large solid white oak door with a golden face of a lioness with a knocker hanging from its mouth. O'Conner steps up to the door, the knockers' eyes are peepholes for the resident to see whose coming. O'Conner smiles and begins to pull the brass ring; just as he raises the knocker, the door opens. "Hi, I'm Roy." "Hello, I'm Jamie, agent for Starrlight." They shake hands as Roy holds out his left arm, "Come on in, have a look around." Stepping in, O'Connor's taken by the eloquence, "Is this Savonnerie carpet?" "Yep." "Wow, this is nice." After touring the apartment, they sit at his desk, where Roy hands him the contract.

Roy smiles, "Here's the lease and all you have to do is get this to me, and I will submit you the keys to the apartment and mailbox." O'Conner questions, "Where's the box located?" "Oh, they are inside in the lobby on the far side towards the front." "How does the post man deliver?" "They have an electronic key to the gate and the box is built into the wall outside." O'Conner rubs his chin, "I must have missed the mailbox, I didn't see it out front." Roy smiles, "Well, it's the brass shield hanging on the front of the building." O'Conner's surprised, "Are you serious, wow, I thought that was part of the decoration." "Well that's the idea; if you take a look at the top of the shield, you will see a key hole, that's how the mail man gets access to our boxes. There's also a slot under the key hole, where people can place misrouted mail."

After a brief run through, O'Conner stands, "Thanks Mr. Johnson, I'll get this back to you on Friday." "I tell you what, if you can fax me a copy of it by tomorrow, then I'll give you your box key today, where you will find the keys to the apartment. It will be in a blue envelope; these envelopes are used for the residents only, and the mail carrier knows not to touch them. I can get the original lease when I return from out of town." O'Conner's interested, "Oh, you're leaving?" "Well, I plan on going on a little trip, and there's a great chance that I may not be here on Friday. "Oh, I see; so, since I'm headed to New York tonight, I'm sure I can get her to sign this, then I will fax it first thing in the morning."

Roy shows O'Conner the front entrance. "You have to use this electric key to leave and get in. All you have to do is have it on your person, and the door will automatically open for you. This key will be in your box when you fax me." The thought hits Roy, "Oh yeah; the guards shift is from eleven to seven each night. They wear suits or white tuxedos and they are licensed to carry a concealed weapon." "Yes, I read your ad; that's really neat, I'm sure that gives your residence extra security." Roy continues, "They also assist in parking, and in the case of party situations, both our guys work that same night." "That sounds good." Roy hands O'Conner the key and shakes his hand, "Thanks, and congratulations on your hit, Never Bend a Buck." O'Conner smiles, "Thank you." He leaves.

Nine O'clock, morning, the screeching sound of the fax machine echoes through the unfurnished apartment, where sits Roy, who gazes out into the blistering heat; it's going to be a big day on the beach. The machine halts, Roy smiles, he knows it's the signed lease from Starrlight. The clock reaches five minutes after, the voice of mystery rings into his ears. He has the song in his head, but he can't make out who sang the song; the still voice calls, soft whispers of desire set the kindle wood in his heart a blaze. It's on the tip of his tongue, but he can't make it out. As it melts away at his conscience, the fire grows, pulling him like a moth in the dark, drawn to the light. It eats his soul like worms boring out of an apples core. Not able to hold it back, the thirst for understanding overloads his experience; He yearns for completeness; there must be closure. Not knowing something when you know you should know something is an appalling feeling no one wants. The same question that has gripped men's throats since time began squeezes the air out of him. Beside himself, Roy challenges the burning quest; "Why am I here?"

Roy rushes as he files the lease and leaves a message for Blacksmith to take his computers and accessories to his apartment. "Yes, I want to fly out today." The travel agent responds, "Is this business or pleasure?" A serious voice speaks, "Business." "And where to Mr. Johnson?" "Egypt." "Egypt?" "Yeah, Egypt. How soon can you have me headed out?" The agent finds an opening.

"I see in our records that you've gotten your passports, do you have your passport on you Mr. Johnson?" "Yes, I have everything." "Yes, Mr. Johnson, I remember you now; sorry about that Captain. Okay, let's see, well, I have an international flight for Cairo Egypt headed out at ten, is that too soon?" "No, book me; I'm going out the door now." "Okay, I will put you in; so, are you leaving out now?" "Yes." "Alright, then is it okay for me to call you on your cell for your conformation number?" "Yes." "And again, we thank you for using Sweet Vacations Express; it will take about a half hour to clear, and from there, we will give you the conformation just in case you have a problem. Have a nice flight Mr. Johnson." "Okay, thank you Vickie."

Like a child who runs late for his first big performance, Roy darts out the complex and jumps in the taxi; it's the same driver from before. "Where to man?" Plunging into the back seat he hastily speaks, "I hope you're wearing your lead foot today, because I have thirty minutes before my flight, and I have a thousand dollar bill that says I'll make it." The taxi driver looks up through his rear view mirror and winks, "Gotcha." the cab spins off. Roy makes the flight and carries one brown leather bag. He looks at his ticket, which displays eighteen hours and thirty-five minutes of flight before he reaches Cairo Egypt.

Seventeen hours and one minute, Roy stares out the window of endless darkness. That's just it; what's darkness for one's eyes is light for another. Small molecules bounce off the airplanes window. The shiny material amuses Roy as it dances the dance of billions of bouncing marbles. In the distance, Roy sees it; a massive cloud stretching for what looks like miles. He turns and looks toward the seat across to see if anyone else is aware of the phenomenon; everyone's asleep, besides, he was sure that it was way too dark for any normal person to see. He glances back at the large puffy grey-black clouds. Again, his eyes catch the wonder, of what appears as a bubble or angled glass surrounding large crystal like high risers. Unbelievable to his eyes, Roy rubs them and looks harder; Due to the thickness of the clouds, he's not able to make out all the details. Five minutes, and the glory disappears into the thickness of night. Roy could feel the hairs on the back of his neck raise. He's not sure if he was dreaming with his eyes open, or actually experiencing something beyond belief. He whispers to himself, "It looked like a city." Nodding, Roy lays his head back into his seat and watches the movie Never Bend a Buck.

At the end of the flight, Roy watches the last episode of the movie and notices the molecules inside the television screen. A white light appears; it quickly flashes the beautiful illuming face of a woman, which resembles the same angelic creature encountered in Giza. His heart races as he veers closer to see; But the image is gone. Three dark shadows streak across the monitor, followed shortly by a large white lightning bolt. Roy's able to make out the flash of lightning; it is a male figure with a trumpet in its hand followed by several short blasts of lights, which appeared to be men in white priestly robes.

One of the creatures, which followed the male figure with the trumpet, stops, and begins to glance at Roy from the opposite side of the screen. It tilts its head as if in awe that Roy was able to see it's presence. A high pitched sound pops his ears, it's the stewardess pressing the intercom to announce the arrival of the flight; He shifts his eyes away for a moment, only to look back to an empty television screen, which displays the ending movie credits.

Fifteen minutes till midnight, the time difference annoys some passengers who complain about the long flight. Roy grabs his bag and walks off the plane. It's midnight; He begins his journey southwest towards Giza. The walk is only a few miles. Roy, one mile from the Sphinx, heads outside the souvenir shop, the place where his battle began. The shops closed, as he continues toward his birthmark. An eerie feeling overcomes his mind; he approaches were it all began. Suddenly, his eyes widen; Scaling several feet into the night sky, is a humongous white fig tree. He yells, "This tree wasn't here!" He looks around, making sure of his location. Yes, he's sure that's where he laid when the winged creature attacked him; it was at that very monstrous trunk where he pierced her through. The question races through Roy's mind of how the tree got there. It scales the sky and seems to be as old as Giza, but its leaves are fresh and green like a young plant. Roy marveled; the whole area was desert except for that one tree. He reasons and concludes; there's no way a tree could have grown in such a short time. Roy steps up to the white trunk; the leaves are full of figs the size of baseballs. He grabs a fig and bites into it; the taste is as sweet as honey. He chews the fig to savor the delicacy, and then spits it out; He doesn't want to experience a sick stomach as he did the last time he ate food. He grabs three figs and places them into his bag. The thought goes through his mind that maybe the creatures' blood somehow caused the tree to grow. Roy begins to connect the blood with that of the old scriptures which makes mention of the blood of life. Roy shakes his head in doubt; He ignores the strong message, but is unable to evade the truth, that there's a connection between him and that tree. Roy let's out a long breath, and turns to walk toward the Sphinx. As he nears, stone walls and barbed wire surround the Sphinx. There's several post and towers. He gets close to the wall, and looks through a crack; His heart pounds, he sees it, the Sphinx. His newfound eyes allow him to see the four guards at the entrance.

The urgency beckons Roy to find out what's behind the massive stone door. He speaks under his voice, "I'm going." Not able to contain himself, he drops his bag and dashes around, towards the front gate. He squats down, there they are, the infrared sensors, which would go off if he passes the fencing. As a lion, he waits, hoping to seize a spectacle of opportunity. Looking down at his boots, he remembers his escape from the Foxes Hole. The damaged boots reflects a mishap surrounding his evading the lounge. Taking a deep breath, he looks up and sprints, "Bam!" A flash of lightning flies into the air and hit's the stone door. The guards are in surprise as they look into the sky for clouds. The guards look at each other in shock as one speaks, "Did you see that?" "Yeah, that was lightning." The third replies, "That's what I don't like about being stationed out in the open desert; anything can hit you." Two of the guards stand further under the sphinx to avoid any more lightning strikes.

Inside the Sphinx, Roy stands; He doesn't understand it, but knows he's inside. As he looks around, he notices that he's naked. Underneath his feet are micro fibers of shredded clothes. Roy picks up a piece of molted metal; His boots are disintegrated. None of it fazes him as he ventures around. All he sees is what is left over of a high tech display and dismantled infrared sensor. The writings on the walls are meaningless to him as he frowns at the Egyptian paintings. Although there are many artifacts, he remains unpeeled from his thirst.

"Nothing!" He takes a last look at the paintings and notices one Egyptian who appears several times throughout the Sphinx. The Egyptian wears a mask, which resembles a lions head, holding up a scepter in his right hand while pointing down with his left. Roy turns back, and remembers seeing the rod. In the small room, at the center of the Sphinx, next to the broken high tech display, where once laid the lead box, stands a scepter incased in thick Plexiglas. He draws back his fist, "Crack!" the front splinters, as he pulls the plastic away, giving him access. He pulls the scepter out and examines the inscriptions along its shaft. The six-foot staff is made out of gold, the top resembles a dog and the bottom forms an ohm symbol. He looks at the bottom and figures that it could be used as a lightning rod or conductor of electricity.

Roy examines the paintings on the wall, and returns to the place in front of the staff and holds it up in his right hand while pointing down with his left. After a minute, he exasperates, "This is Stupid!" Turning towards the display, he kicks the splintered display as it flies off the stone foundation. "Clack!" He shoves the staff into the stone holder. The impact of the scepter causes the holder to give way into the ground as the scepter pops all the way in, revealing only the head.

As Roy turns to walk away, he hears small rocks bottom, echoing underneath his feet. His eyes glisten as he turns and hardens his brow. Fixing his eyes on the sunken staff, his heart races as he rushes down onto his knees and pulls. The metal slides against the stone, small pieces crumble, "pop pop pop." Again, he hears the hollow sound. Brushing away the Plexiglas and dust, he leans forward and looks into the hole; It's pitched black. Roy lifts his head away, and takes another look; it's a room underneath. Standing, he paces back and focuses the hole and whips, "Bam!" a flash of lightning arcs into the narrow opening. Roy opens his eyes; Ancient inscription surrounds the walls. The paintings are much like the ones above, except they are Egyptians wearing mask of lions, eagles, horses and locust. On the far east of the room is a star, where stands giant angels with wings.

The west side of the room is a small replica of the Sphinx. He walks to the Sphinx and removes it from its base. There's a stone box overlaid with gold. Roy pulls the top as it gives way and cracks. The seal is broken, revealing rolled up sheepskin. He unravels the scroll of skin. He's not able to make out the writing but is enchanted by the pictures. A large angelic like man stands over a woman who has a child which grows to be a giant with six toes and six fingers. A light bulb goes on in his mind; He remembers the scripture, which speaks of giants born in the earth. The scroll ends with the woman bowing down to her new child. He looks into the Sphinx and finds three more stone boxes. Removing the scrolls, he looks again to see if anything's left. The base has a seam; Roy pulls at the stone and removes a lid, which houses clothes. He rises up black baggy pants, which tie at the waist. The second clothing is a black robe, which pulls over, and the third is a black robe, which wears like a long coat. The feel of the fabric is much like silk but has a coolness like he's never felt before.

Roy's amazed at the condition of the material, which feels like it was just made new. The sweet scent emitting from them sends a smile across his face; this is the same material he felt when he battled the angelic creature. After two hours, Roy puts on the clothes and gathers the scrolls. Not wanting to ruin his new finding, he thinks up a way to get out of the two story underground tomb. Looking up, he jumps, his grip imbeds into the stone as he crawls up the smooth wall. At the hole, he punches upward, causing the stone to give way to a larger exit.

Roy finds a heavy slab and covers the hole he hewed. The challenge rushes his mind as he thinks of ways to leave without being seen. He returns to the main entrance, and sees two pieces of black stripped leather protruding from the corner of the stone; it's what's left of his boots. He pulls the strips out and wraps them around the scrolls. He sees the men's aura through the door, two on the left and two on the right. "Boom!" The stone burst open from the center. The soldiers look around to see what hit them. Darkness covers the fleeing gargoyle, which disappears into the night. He rushes to the front wall, where lays his untouched bag. The lights shine overhead, out into the bliss. The soldiers are looking for terrorist with grenade launchers. Surprised that the infrared fails to detect, Roy lays low in the black robe until the commotion settles. Four thirty rolls around, and two hours of searching comes up with nothing. He waits until the lights shine on the south side. When it's safe, he gazelles through the desert sand until he reaches the main road towards Cairo.

At ten after five, Roy checks into the Pharaoh Egypt Hotel. Pleased, he stays in his room and examines the scrolls. The light fades; the day gives way to night. Fifteen hours has passed; He decides to go down to the lobby. The Concierge notices him, "Excuse me sir, I believe you have a message." Roy looks around and points at himself, "For me?" "Yes, are you in room twenty one?" "Yes." I have a message from a Michelle." Roy glances at the note; it's in Arabic. "I can't read this." The Concierge looks, oh, I'm sorry, but the person spoke in Arabic. Do you want me to read it for you?" "Go ahead." The Concierge reads, "I believe I left my lighter with you, if you could, please leave it at the front desk." A question mark smacks him, "No, you have the wrong guy. I don't know anyone here." The Concierge looks puzzled, "Are you sure?" "Yeah, I am very sure." Roy walks outside to get a breath of fresh air.

*

The Terror of Legion

T he werewolf stands off its fours and walks into the Mohammed Mahmoud Khalil Mansion. Underneath, lays the Hall of Pharaohs. Behind the antique desk sets a black oak kings chair, where sits in brown military camouflage and black beret, Dracula, Lord of Vampires. Tearing down the stairs, breaking vases, the growls of the werewolf echoes through the corridors. The double black oak doors fly open; Foam bubbles from his mouth while catching his breath.

Standing on each side of the desk is Connie and the grey eyed Albino. Dracula speaks, "You're getting blood on my carpet." The sound of several distraught voices projects in unison, "Where is it?" Dracula responds, "I told you I would deliver the head to you when you complete your task." As its teeth snarls, the eyes of the werewolf angers, "I'll rip your head, off!" The massive paws swipes, "Bam!" A statue head flies across the room and lands against the bookcase. Dracula sighs, "From the looks of it, you're not going to last." The werewolf looks down at his bullet wounds; he knows that he will die soon. Dracula pours a glass of red wine into a gold goblet with rubies and takes a drink. Setting the goblet down, he smirks while looking up, "Now I'm asking the questions." He let's out a short breath, "Legion, we have known each other for over two thousand years now, and I have never seen you quite this desperate. You know our pack, you deliver the goods and I supply your needs. It's a give and take relationship; you know that. You can't just go around useless, destroying everything you see, or is it just your nature; Why of course it's your nature, you will never see it my way, your kind never does."

The werewolf falls onto its fours, it weakens from lost blood. Panting, it raises its head and gasp, "We will prevail!" Dracula continues, "I thought you worked together as one. How come one of you come to my club and smashes my suite, costing me an untimely bill?" Legion stands, "We are many, we never separate!"

Dracula's surprised of the strength bestowed by the werewolf. He knows that Legion is not responsible for the havoc made at his lounge. "So, I see that you are still intact. I had to know, because your kind doesn't all stick together. Find me the Gargoyle and I will deliver you the head. I know you have ways of knowing; so why don't you use your gifts?" "Roar!" Legion heckles through the curdling blood from his mouth. His grotesque laughter echoes the halls, "We will go in her!" Dracula interrupts, "No, not Connie." Legion looks at the Albino, "Then we will enter him!" Dracula looks at the Albino, "Him? Oh, I'm sorry, you've just met, this is my leading man..." Legion interrupts and stares at the Albino, "I know who you are, Xan Bledsoe, leader of the secret nations, master of the Foxes Hole!" Dracula's impressed, "I see there are no strangers in your presence, Legion; But you can't have this one, he's my strongest and most prized, it would be a waste for you to destroy his mind." Dracula nods at Connie, who radios two soon-to-be vampires, who's affected by her virus. In steps two tall men, holding the arms of Sarah from the lounge, it is Dan Gordon and Kyle Theodore Hutchinson.

Sarah stands between the men in obedience. "You see now, One of my prizes just went bad. It seems she has failed her last job assignment and she is in need of being placed. She is far stronger than these two men are, and yet, as placid as a lamb. Such beauty, but the strength of her legs could drop the strongest of men. When I saw Sarah perform in the Olympics, I just had to have her; so I bit her. My own prize possession, just like Connie and Xan. But now, the taste of rotten blood spoils my appetite." Dracula stands as his breath hits Sarah's face, "Family always stick together!"

Dracula's disappointed that Sarah was not around when Roy fought in the suites. Tears flow from her silent face. Her eyes, fixed on Dracula, never shifts or falls in shame. Dracula walks over towards the bookcase were stands knights armor. He pulls a sword from the knight's sheath and walks toward her. Sarah holds in her sound as she swallows her fate. He looks at her with the sword drawn in his left arm. Sarah has respect for him, her peaceful eyes overcomes the terror, as she looks him in his eyes and calmly speaks, "I'm not afraid to die."

Dracula smiles as he turns his body while still facing her, "I know sweetie, you are one of the most honorable children I have ever spawned." He walks in a circle as his head turns again and looks, "You are my daughter, and just like in any family, there comes a time when family breaks up or moves on; in some cases it's love and in others, its hate. In this case, it is a marriage, a marriage between two persons. This is a romance between Romeo and Juliet. The sorrow of this plot is that Romeo has to die." He walks over to the werewolf and hands him the sword. The werewolf staggers toward Sarah as Gordon and Hutchinson grabs her arms. He lifts the sword; Sarah accepts her fate and closes her eyes, "Swish, thump!" He severs his own head. Blood gushes out the stem of his neck while the body drops a lifeless spasm. The thumping sound of the rolling head causes her to lift her eyes to a downed werewolf. The shock of the horror sends chills up her spine as she tries to understand what happened. Suddenly, a loud shrill emits from its neck; A thousand dark shadows begins to lift, as they fill the emptiness below the ceiling. Sarah eyes fill with fear, she now believes the rumors of the thousand demons of terror. She begins to panic and jerks her arms in an effort to break their grip. As they hold her, the quietness is broken as she looks to Dracula and begs, "Kill me, kill me, don't let this happen to me, please, please, kill me!"

Sarah snags Hutchinsons collar and flips him across the desk. Gordon tries to grab her other hand as she kicks, "Thump!" he topples the bookcase. Her eyes fix upward, she dashes for the two doors. Connie starts after her, but Dracula raises his hand, "No, let him earn this one." The demons fly out behind the fleeing vampire. Dracula looks to the others, "If she escapes, then she's earned back her right to the blood line."

Sarah's fast, as she races down Riverside. Legion closes in; she jumps across a high wall, pulls away, leaving him in her dust. One mile down the road, her legs zoom past several tourists. They are amazed at her speed, one familiarly recognizes, "Hey, that looked like Sarah Callaway, she won a gold two years ago."

Sarah passes a car at thirty-five miles an hour and enters a park where an elderly American woman walks her white poodle. The trees rattle, Sarah is overrun by Legion. She falls and rolls on the ground while screaming, "No, don't, no no no!" The swarm overshadows her as she frantically kicks around. She screams while ripping off her red dress and bra, "Ah-ah-ah!" The elderly woman ties her dog to the park bench and runs over to see, "Are you okay honey, what's wrong?" She watches as Sarah kicks, twist and turns while screaming. The lady looks around to see if anyone could help, but there's no one in sight. Sarah's eyes roll into her head, she spits and cries. The elderly woman steps closer and leans over her bare breast to see if there's an injury; Sarah moans in pain. She quickly opens her eyes, grabs her own forearm, and bites into it. The elderly woman's shocked, "Oh my god, she's crazy!" Sarah jumps onto her feet and captures the fleeing elderly. She quickly spins the woman around and tares her blouse off exposing her girdle. She pounces the woman and rips her juggler vein from her neck. She mounts the woman and drinks the spouting blood; the woman dies.

An enraged poodle tied to the bench drowns out the slurping sound. Sarah looks up and approaches the snapping poodle. She reaches for the leash, but the poodle nips Sarah's finger. "Bitch!" She jumps down; the poodle goes for her neck. The poodle makes a short loud screech and goes limp. Its neck's clutched in the mouth of a hungry vampire; she rises, as the poodle plops to the ground.

Sarah snatches off her panties and eats them. She begins to dance in circles while pulling out chunks of her hair. She approaches a boat on the river and springs onto the deck, and lands where a couple makes out to rock and roll in the lower cabin. She jumps down and pulls the man off the woman; His neck snaps. She lunges towards the woman and bites off her nipple. She breaks the woman's neck and gouges out her eyes, eating them. Sarah screams and is heard a mile away. The tour bus calls and reports the unusual sound to local police.

In Giza, the naked vampire walks into the souvenir shop. The Egyptian elder's speechless. A beautiful attractive woman covered in blood walks to the counter and points to the sword. Two patrons walk out, "Nasty whore." "Um, are you okay?" She gives him an enchanting look. "Is that real blood?" A low clicking sound chatters out of her mouth.

The Egyptian grabs the sword and points it in her face. "You bloody American, get out, now!" Sarah grabs the end of the sword, yanking it out of the Egyptians hands; "Pop." the sword goes into her mid section. She pushes it through her stomach, causing it to come out her lower side. The Egyptian yells, "Holy shit!" He urinates on himself. She turns and shows him her back; she doesn't bleed. He panics, "Oh god, oh god!" She faces him, pulls the sword out, and looks at the sign on the wall, "Koluo thura." The Egyptian nervously replies, "It means, angels watching over." Her voice, sounding like several men, speaks, "No, weed brain; It means forbidden entrance. It's used to keep Angelos out. We are not Angelos; we are Legion." She kicks the displays over, breaking everything in her path. The Egyptian darts for the door. She tares the place apart in search for the flaming sword. The wild screams is heard by the Egyptian who runs towards the soldiers at the Sphinx.

The door breaks open, Sarah runs out with the stone tablet in her hands. She catches the Egyptian, causing him to loose footing as he falls on his side. She jumps on him and rolls him to his back. She breaks the stone tablet and shoves pieces into his mouth. Eat the words of death!" The Egyptian chokes and dies. Setting her eyes at the Sphinx, Sarah runs in fury. As she approaches, the soldiers place the spotlight on her and tell her to stop. She cries, "They raped me, help, they raped me!" The soldier looks through his night vision, "It's a naked woman running towards us." The other responds, "What's the sensors show?" "Nothing, she's not wired." "Radio the gate, but don't' let her in. If she needs help, then call the locals; they'll handle it." Sarah's met at the gate by twelve armed soldiers. A hummer pulls up behind her. She yells, "Bitch fucking ass trooper!"

The soldiers command Sarah to lay face down on the ground. Two men step out of the hummer, to make sure she's not carrying any ammo. "Clear." One soldier holds out a blanket to cover her, while the other keeps his machine gun pointed at her. She suddenly flips around and snatches his weapon, shoving it into her vagina, "Fuck me, fuck me!" The soldier manages to grab his weapon from her as the other tries to hold her down and cover her. "God damn, she's cocky as hell!" The soldiers behind the gate burst out, "Ha ha ha!" "No, I'm serious; I can't keep this bitch down!"

The Sergeant orders two others, "Get over there and help him." They leave their weapons and run over to assist. Sarah yells as they wrestle her. "Grab her arms." "Get her legs." As they lift her up, she pulls and yanks, squirming, "Ah, no-oo!" Her arms and legs flinches in and out, as the four soldiers hardly contain her.

The Sergeant's dumbfounded, "You've got to be kidding me. John, David, get in there!" The two soldiers head to pick her up by her midsection. In sudden motion, a soldier screams, his ear soars, hitting a soldier behind the gate. Another cry out and falls back, his hearts ripped from his chest. She simultaneously snaps necks as two flop to the ground.

"Bam!" John flies against the hummer. Two soldiers in the hummer start the engine as David runs for the door. Sarah snatches him out of the door, he bends over screaming, his pants are blood filled at the crotch. Sarah turns and looks at the Sergeant behind the gate and spits out a bloody penis. Her quick movements spell bounded the soldiers at the gate, the Sergeant commands, "Fire!" bullets fly into the dark while Sarah jumps inside the hummer and kills the other two. The hummer peels into the night, the soldiers are left behind to taste the dust of death.

Roy, in the lobby, sits and watches the tourist walk by; statues and design of the Pharaoh Egypt Hotel fascinate them. An American man sits on the leather chair, glances over and asks, "You mind if I turn the channel? I can't understand this Arabic crap." "No, go right ahead, I wasn't watching the television anyway." The man flips the station; the reporter breaks the news, "We have breaking news; The Oasis Hotel was attacked tonight by terrorist, killing eighty persons, twelve were American. Only one survive as what appears as an American Caucasian woman; She's last seen on security surveillance, nude, covered in blood and running through this glass door. There's still question of her identity and her whereabouts." The man curses, "Are you serious, well, there goes our vacation!" Roy's eyes catches the blur, he sees the demons outlining illuminating Sarah, while she crashes out the hotels entrance. Roy picks up the remote, looks over at the man, "Do you mind if I change it for a minute?" "Sure, go right ahead pal." As he scans the stations to find another coverage, the man ask, "So, you have family here?"

Roy responds, "Naw, I'm here on business." "Really, what's your job?" He scrambles an answer, "I collect artifacts." "Wow, that must be interesting; so you're an anthropologist?" "Well, no, I am a paleontologist." The man squints, "Well isn't that the same?" "Naw, I don't dig for fossils, I research ancient earth history and archeological findings." The man nods, "Oh, you help anthropologist." Roy, not paying the man much attention, nods while flipping stations. The man demands a verbal answer, "So, I said does that mean you help anthropologist?" Roy quickly glances over and looks back at the television, "Yeah, something like that."

The channel flicks pass the news, Roy clicks back, it's another reporter talking, "...Right here and crashes through this door." He looks and is certain of the unusual shadow surrounding the woman. He turns to the man, "Hey." "Yeah?" "Could you see any lights or smoke coming off that girl?" "Are you joking?" "No, I'm serious." The man shakes his head and makes a confused face. "No, I mean the pictures a little blurry, but I couldn't see anything." Roy looks and stands, "That's what I thought." "Are you okay?" "Yeah, I just need my glasses, cause I could see lights around the woman." "Yeah, it sounds like you do need your glasses."

Roy starts toward the stairs as he waves, "See ya later." "Okay guy, it's been nice to meet you." The Concierge makes an announcement, "This message just came in from the authorities, no one is allowed to leave tonight. There are no flights out of Cairo tonight, so if you are scheduled to fly out, then you will have to stay until tomorrow afternoon. For your safety, there will be military escorts to and from the airport. If you have any questions, please feel free to come to the desk or call this number." Frustrated and disappointed, some people boo the announcer. Roy turns and briskly walks to the counter, "Hey, when did you say we could fly out?" Responding, the Concierge lifts his eyebrows, "Well, I was told that there are no flights tonight, not until tomorrow after noon." Roy speaks for the frustrated people waiting behind him, "And what about all the people who paid for a hotel tonight, just to see the city before they fly out tomorrow?" "I'm sorry sir, but that's just how it goes, you are welcomed to call this number here if you have questions." Roy hit's the counter, "Well that's just bullshit!" The Concierge speaks up, "Where, where are you going?" "I'm getting the hell out of here, that's where I'm going." "You can't leave sir."

Roy stops in his tracks and turns, "What the hell can you do about it? Not a damned thing, bye!" The scrawny unarmed security guard at the door steps out of Roy's way, which passes and disappears into the night. The sky's full of military helicopters circling overhead; the streets are empty, terror is on the loose. Roy marches along side the Nile; he smells blood in the air. The police are everywhere; it's hard to get from one place to another without proper identification. He walks toward a park and is stopped by officers, "Do you have I.D.?" "Yeah." "Pull it out please." He reaches his back pocket, opens his wallet and hands it to the officer. The officer looks it over and hands it back, "Thank you Captain, you may pass."

The police are at the crime scene; it's the old lady and her maimed dog. The smell of death brings an electric shock to his tongue.

Roy feels eyes watching him. He walks pass the deceased lady to where the dog lays; a light catches his eye. He's seen it before, It's the same electrical feeling he experience when he came out the souvenir shop. As he starts toward the light, a warm feeling overflows his veins; the same feeling a person gets when they are sexually aroused. As he approaches the light, which sets between the trees, he stops to catch his heart. "Damn." His mind trips, he wonders if he was getting his kicks off seeing the dog and the old lady, or was it his pursuit of the light. "Naw." He shakes it off, and looks up; the light is gone. He scans the trees and bushes for the light, but something else catches his attention. It's the smell; the same smell he smelt at the airport, but worst. He jumps across the wall and heads for the smell. Low chattering bounces the wall as he closes in on the Niles banks.

There she is; Sarah rolls on the ground. "Swish." The fishing knife in her hand slices her legs and arms. Suddenly, she jumps into a crouching position; she knows he watches. Sarah looks up the bank side and calls, "Bazyli!" He anticipates her move and jumps down to the landing. Sarah springs like a jackrabbit; the chase is on. Tearing through bushes and sand, Sarah stops and turns. Roy closes in, as she leaps towards him. "Thump!" She lands in his arms, her hands moves back and forth at his face and back, in rage.

Roy's natural reflex catches a swift hand stabbing his face and shoulder. In shock, he manages to unlock her left arm from his neck. Her feet lands on the ground in front of him while simultaneously slicing his face and chest. "Yah, yah, yah!"

Roy tucks his head from furious strikes. The yelling sound stops, he looks up to Sarah who's staring at the bent blade. He glances down at his chest where the blade landed, nothing, not a scratch. Lounging forward, she screams. He goes to the ground; the ravenous mad woman mounts him. Her jaws lock onto his neck; she holds him in a chokehold while biting. Roy flips her onto her back; he's on top. Her face still grips his neck as he uses his hands to pull back her hair. Deep growling reverberates from her mouth as he shoves the back of her head into the sand. The slapping of his face and torso cracks the night air. She's extremely accurate at hitting him, her nails claws his face and arms; His body never scars. His eyes widen, he's surprised at her strength and quickness. Matching her speed, he grabs her arms and pushes them over her head. She squirms and shakes as Roy presses his knees against her sides. She spits into his face and yells out, "Bitch, fucking bitch!" Roy over yells, "Shut up!" Sarah begins to make squealing noises. He knows its Sarah; she's much stronger than the last time he held her down. He smells it, and sees them. Legions voice projects from her, "Bazyli! You come to kill us before our time?" Roy's eyes glimmer; he feels the strong magnetism of familiarity.

Roy sees the demons in Sarah's face, "Who are you?" The voice responds, "I know who you are." he questions, "Oh yeah?" "You're Bazyli of Angelos." Roy tightens his grip, "What the hell does that mean?" Legion laughs, "Why did you come before the time?" Roy frowns and slaps her arms against the sand, "What's that?" "I know who you are." He speaks through his grinded teeth, "Then who am I? "You're Gargoyle." He sights hundreds of dark faces in Sarah. "What does that mean, I don't understand that. Speak up, who am I?" "You are Royal, Gargoyle of Angelos." He figures Legion knows his name through Sarah." "What the hell is a Gargoyle?" "Asim." "What's Asim?" "You are Asim!" "What's Asim?" "Guardian of man, watcher of spirits. Are you come to kill us Bazyli?"

Roy grabs her neck and squeezes. Legion gasps for air, "Let us go." Roy grits his teeth, "Let her go first." "We cannot let her go." "Why can't you let her go?" "Because you have us by our neck." "So, if I kill her, then you die?" "Please, do not kill us before the time." "Before what time?" There's a pause of silence. Roy squeezes harder, as Legion strains, "Before Armageddon." Roy's in shock, he denies his ears. His grip tightens, as his eyes focuses into the ground, which appears to open up, and absorbs part of the demons.

As Roy loosens her neck, the darkness from under Sarah begins to close up, allowing legion to return into her face. Roy squeezes again, the demons begin to suck into the darkness under the ground. Legion pleads, "We beg you, release us and we will leave her." His hands open, the clutch of death releases, Roy stands.

Sarah sits up and vomits blood; Legion ascends out of her. Surrounding Roy is a thousand red-eyed dark demons. They are ugly and stink like sulfur. They hover in the darkness of the night. They look around as if they were looking for something. Suddenly, at once, they fly away, above the trees, into the streetlight; the bulb pops, Legion's gone.

Sarah sits in a pool of blood, she blinks a blank stare; she has no idea where she is. Roy squats down and looks into her eyes, he can see her aura, peaceful and content. "What happened Sarah?" "He was after me." "Who?" "Legion." "What happened after that?" "I don't know." tears flow down her eyes. Roy repeats, "What happened next Sarah?" She weeps out of control, "I don't know, I don't know." Roy stands; he knows she's telling the truth. He steps over her, "You smell." He grabs her ankles, drags her to the riverside and slings her in, "Take a bath." She yells, "Ah!" Her body splashes in, headfirst. Sarah comes up for air. With her hands across her shoulders, her elbows cover her breast as she shivers in the wet coldness. Roy yells, "I said get that shit off you!" Sarah's head shakes, she looks at her arms and hair matted in blood. She washes herself through whimpers of shock; the vampires awake. He commands, "Turn around. Go under one more time." Sarah dips her head under the water and comes up. "Again." She dips and comes up again. "Turn around, hold your head down." Shivering, she bows. He sees she's clean. "Okay, get out of the water." Sarah walks towards him. "Stop right there." Roy takes off his torn shirt, revealing his tank top. "Put this on." The long shirt covers her down to her thighs.

"Did you follow me here?" "No." "Then how did you get here Sarah?" "I booked a flight." "What for?" "Because I didn't kill you." Roy slaps her face; she holds her head down, and then looks up. "So, you did follow me." "No, I didn't." He raises his fist, "What's keeping me from killing you right now?" "I don't know, I think you should kill me." She looses her composure, "Do it, do it! If anybody should kill me, it should be you." Roy swings his fist, but holds it, stopping right at her face. The wind from his fist raises her damp hair; she doesn't blink.

"Why didn't you kill me Mr. Johnson?" Roy lets his arms down and responds, "Because, in my eyes, you're already dead." He turns and walks away. Sarah yells out, "You think I like being like this, well I don't!" She looks around and follows behind his brisk pace. "Slow down Mr. Johnson, please, let me explain." He turns, "The next time I see you, you won't like it." She holds her arms up, "So, what am I to do now?" "Go back the way you came." "I'm already dead Mr. Johnson. If I go back, they are going to kill me." "Well, you said you wanted to die, what better way to die then by your own."

A block away from his hotel, Roy stops in his tracks. He knows she's followed him at a distance. "I know you're behind me Sarah. Why don't you go back?" He turns around, the wind blows her nappy black hair, she speaks, "I'm scared." Roy lets out a gasp, "I can't believe this. You're willing to die by my hands, but you're scared to die by your own. Who are you afraid of?" She cries, "Legion!" Sarah breaks down; she's felt the terror inside. She falls on her knees and holds her stomach while rocking. "Please help me." Roy walks over and snatches her up. "I ain't helping you, you have to help yourself." He looks into her eyes. He thinks of the way he acted towards Missti before he left Womack. "Come on." He goes to the door. The security guard's on duty. Roy looks at her, "Act passed out." He picks her up in his arms and waits. Security lets a couple in and returns to the door. Another person goes to the door, "Zoom." Roy carries her through the door just before it shuts. No one sees, as he zips up the stairs; the door opens. Roy lets Sarah down. "You stay here; I have to get some water." Sarah goes in.

At the front desk, He walks by but is interrupted, "Excuse me. Are you Mr. Johnson from room twenty one?" "Yeah, that's me. Oh, a very pretty woman came by looking for you." Roy thinks that his night couldn't get any weirder. "Oh yeah, who?" The woman looks into the log, well, let me see it was, a, Michelle." "I told you guys that I didn't know anybody named Michelle. What did she look like?" The woman nods, "Well, you're going to have to ask Emad, he's the one who saw her and took the message." "When does Emad come in?" She looks into the log. "His schedule's tomorrow evening at five." "Well, I hope I'm gone before then." The woman has a puzzled look, "Are you aware of the flight situation?" Roy interrupts, "Yeah, yeah, I know all about the terrorist crap." He walks to the dining area to get more bottled water.

The night is long, morning awaits. Sarah sleeps in Roy's bed; the lights are off at the bed, but the televisions running in the small living room with kitchenette. Roy sits on the limestone coffee table. While staring at her silent slumber, He counts the number of beats her heart makes per minute. Roy watches, he can almost see what she dreams. It gives him a sort of pleasure. The digital clock hits three in the morning. He picks up the remote and mutes the television, and lifts the receiver on the telephone; it didn't ring. Silence is on the other end but he knows someone is there, he feels it, "Hello?" The voice of a woman speaks, "Hi." The softness of her voice soothes his ears, "Hey. Who is this?" She responds, "Is this Roy?" "Yeah, is this Michelle?" No answer. "Are you the one who left me the message?" "Yes." "I'm sorry miss, but you have the wrong guy. I don't have your lighter." Silence, then a soft voice speaks, "Why do you say you don't have my lighter?" "Because I just don't have it. I don't even smoke." "I've seen you smoke." Roy's amused, "Oh really now? Where did you see me smoke?" "Outside." "Outside? Hell, anybody could make that up. What's your name?" No response, He doesn't hear her breathe. He tries to figure out who would know him there. The kindness in her voice makes him wonder if it is a prank call from a friend or affiliate. "Is this a friend of Henry?" Silence continues, "Is this Missti?" A couple of seconds of silence and then, "No, I'm not Missti." "So, you are Michelle, is that right? Well I don't want to be rude, but I don't know any body named Michelle, and as much as you want me to have your lighter, well, I just don't. Maybe somebody else got it."

Roy scrambles his mind. He looks over at Sarah. The woman speaks, "She's not clean." Roy looks down and shakes his head, "What?" "She's unclean." He glances up at Sarah and switches the phone to his other ear. "Do we know each other? I mean, you sound familiar, I just can't put my finger on it yet." She reacts, "How do you like it as I seem familiar to you?" "What do you mean, how do I like it? Is that something I'm supposed to like? "Listen, I am sure you are sleepy, and as much as I'd like to spend this time with you in this sick little game of talk, I should get off of here." "I'm not sleepy." "Well, you should be sleepy, damn; it's after three in the morning. Are you from the front desk?" "No." Listen, if I really did have your lighter, I'd give it to you, just so you could get off my back about it." She responds, "Do you promise?"

Roy laughs, "Sure, I promise." She replies, "Fair enough." "So does

94

this mean you are going to stop calling?" "How do you feel if I stop calling?" "What do you mean, how do I feel if you stop calling, hell, I'd like it if you stop calling. I mean, you only called me once, right? But, I would like this to stop, and I really hope you get your lighter and it's been nice talking to you Michelle, Okay?" Silence smacks Roy in the face, her comforting tone utters, "Okay." Roy speaks in a soft high pitch, "So, this is the part where I say good bye and you say good bye, okay?" "Okay." "Alright, goodnight." Roy waits through the stillness as the gentleness of her voice resonate his ear, "Okay, see you later." Roy hangs up. "Damn, that's crazy."

Sarah's still sleep, but twist and turns from the sun, which peaks through the window. Roy gets up; he's been staring at Sarah all night. She wasn't on his mind; it was the woman on the phone. Roy covers the window with a blanket. He knows that Sarah's fair skin is sensitive to light. The shower looks solid enough to hold Roy. He gets in and cleans up for the day. After dressing, Roy goes down to the gift store to purchase some shoes and clothes for Sarah. He buys himself some slippers; it's the only thing that comes to his mind, at least until he gets back to Los Angeles. Roy buys sweat clothes and women's underwear and bra. He's sure it's the right size for Sarah. He walks in the room; she still sleeps. He knows he should be reacting different, but he seems to shelter her. After all, she's killed many people; He shrugs it off. The Gargoyle doesn't interfere with certain things. He arranges for her to fly to Texas, where her aunt lives.

The flight leaves at four and heads for America; Seated next to Roy in the first class private section, Sarah wears a long sleeve purple sweat shirt and pants and baseball cap with sunscreen on her face and hands. "Thanks for buying my ticket, I owe you my life." Roy smiles. "Sarah?" "Yes, Mr. Johnson." "No, call me Roy. "Okay." "You can do me a favor. I want you to tell me everything I need to know about your kind." She glances at Roy, who appears to be leaning forward, as if he was not sitting all the way back. "Well, what do you want to know?" "I want to know everything. Where do you eat, sleep, how do you survive, what do you like, dislike, how did you get to be in your situation?" She glances over at Roy, who starts to ease back, making sure he doesn't break the seat. A tear flows from her eyes. She starts, "I got the virus after the games in Italy. But it was in Los Angeles where I met him." Roy looks, "who?"

Sarah looks at Roy and lets out a long breath, "I won four gold medals for the United States, that's when I met Draconus. His real name's Kavin, Kavin Drakon. Somehow, after the games, he came to my hotel, and in the lobby, he did it to me. I don't know how to explain it, but he touched me with his eyes. Somehow, he persuaded me to take him to my room. That's when he seduced me. I didn't know it until it was too late. He bit me on my naval. He sucked harder and harder. I didn't even know I was losing blood, it just felt good; I guess it was the wine. After an hour, I started to get very dizzy, I knew something was wrong, but I passed out. When I woke up, I knew something had changed in me. There was a tattoo and two puncher wounds on my navel. I asked my friends how I got them; they told me that the people I left with tried to stop me from getting my navel pierced, because I was drunk. All I know is that from that day forward, I noticed that I wasn't the same."

Roy looks, "What do you mean, not the same?" "After that year in Italy, I began to advance in everything. No one was faster or stronger. One of the first things I noticed was how I walked. It was so easy to walk in heels; Hell, I never wore heels in my life. My legs, I have never had nice legs like this; That's the number one thing about us, our legs, most of us have very gorgeous legs." She looks at him, "Even the men do. We love to strut our stuff; We can't help it, it's just our nature."

Sarah looks at Roy and grabs her finger, "Watch this." "Snap." she breaks her pinky. Roy's eyes get big, "Damn, didn't that hurt?" "Of course it hurt. By the time this flight is over, I'll be able to move my pinky. Just wait, you'll see. Contortion doesn't run in any of my family, but I can place my foot behind my head. I can twist my hand around like this." Sarah bends her hands. "There's something else you should know about us; fucking. We love sex, not just male and female, I mean, we love it in any and every kind of way; it doesn't matter. When I first saw you, all I could think about doing was getting you down and…Well, you know; I am addicted to it; all vampires are. That next year in Los Angeles at the games, I won six medals, all of them gold. Every time I'd go to the beach, I would get very sick and break out in horrible rashes. Two years ago, we were to compete in Atlanta, but you know what happened, I passed out from heat exhaustion. It became national news that I couldn't perform, because I had a rare disease. They tried to say that I also had an advanced form of melanoma."

Sarah Continues, "They said I would die in three months; that's when I went into hiding. The world thought that my family hid me from the public eye so that they could bury me. There's nothing like reading in the papers about your own death. Faking my death seemed easier. Everyone saw me as the pretty brown-eyed blonde who was the champion of champions. I've always had black hair, so I let it grow out. As for my eyes, well, the virus changed my pigmentation. I would wear brown contacts during the games to hide their true color; you can see their blue now. Well, my fair skin, thick clothes, especially leather, helps keep the ultra violet rays off."

Sarah takes a breath, "It was in Atlanta where I met Connie, she challenged me to a race, and won. I was so impressed, that I was willing to hear anything she had to say. From there, she began mentoring me on how to take care of my skin. She offered me a job at the Foxes Tail Lounge, that's when I saw Kavin again. My first night of work, they gave me a room in one of his suites. He told me that he was Dracula, Lord of Vampires and that I could never lead the normal life." She tears up, "So, you want to know all about how it is to be like this? Well, it sucks, I can't sunbathe, but I can go out, I have to wear leather or some kind of sun block. Bright lights stress me out. As far as eating goes, well, we love wine, especially red wine. I only tried wine once that night with Kavin, but ever since then I have to have it. I never ate rare meat or half-cooked food, but now, it's the only thing I can eat, without getting hungry again. I don't even exercise at all, and I can eat all day long and not gain one ounce of fat. That's the cool part of being like this. It wasn't until last year that I really understood what being a vampire was. I met this guy at the lounge; he was a real jerk. I took him down to a suite and, well, he raped me. The asshole didn't even know that I liked it, and when he was done, I stood up, that's when the bastard punched my face and called me a bitch. He turned around and started out the door, so that's when I jumped on his back. Before I knew it, I had him down on the floor. It's so easy to get to the juggler; it gave me a rush. Connie came in and pulled me off him. I would have killed him. To keep him from dying, she burned his neck with this tattoo." She shows him her naval. "Don't be fooled, all vampires don't have this kind of tattoo, but many of us do. We also love to pierce ourselves." "Why?"

"Well, I don't know; I think it has something to do with not bleeding much. It's almost impossible to get our blood. When I passed out at the games in Atlanta, they took me to the emergency, because my blood was low. The ass-holes had no idea what they were dealing with. The nurse stuck me with the needle seven times; she couldn't find my vein. She really freaked out when she tried to draw blood. The needle just retracted; it scared the hell out of them. That's when my mom had me removed from there. She knew something had changed about me. The second time I bit a guy was at the lounge, I worked with this asshole named Skip, well, he was a jerk too. He kept on and on about how he was a Satan worshipper and that he was a real vampire. His best friend John was pretty cool; I kind of liked him. He was really interested in working for the Lounge, but Xan had him do some weird stuff like make pipe bombs and just practical jokes and pranks. I think Johns a genius, but Skip got to me. One night, I snuck him down into a suite. After we did it, he started on the bull crap about him being a vampire, so I bit the vein next to his testicles. He's so stupid that he asked me for a band-aid. After about three weeks, I noticed the change in him; Eating all the rare meat, the shades. He was not a talker anymore. It was then that I knew I did something terrible; I took away his freedom." Sarah goes into a hard stare. A few seconds pass; she shakes it off, "Well anyway, I promised myself I would never bite another person again. So, when I told you that I never killed anyone, well, it was the truth; that's if you don't count the two guys I bit, but they're still alive; But a killer, It's just not me."

Roy looks seriously at Sarah and remains silent; He knows she doesn't realize what happened in Giza. Her eyes light up, "You know what's also cool; I can lift three hundred pounds." Roy smirks, "Really?" She cheers, "Yeah, and that's three hundred pounds with one arm; that's pretty damned tough." Roy expresses, "What about fangs and turning into bats and sucking peoples blood and all that crap?" She sighs, "No, no, no. That's not right." His face goes serious, "What about sleeping in coffins and well, how do you survive?" Sarah explains, "I sleep just like anybody else. I like chicken and hamburgers too. As you can see, I don't have fangs. I've only seen three vampires with fangs and that's Kavin, Connie and Xan. The rest either have their teeth shaved or made to look like that."

Roy glances, "What about other vampires?" She shakes her head, "You mean, are we all the same?" Roy nods, "Yeah." She replies, "No, we are not all the same." Sarah leans close to his ears, "There are three types, and variations within those types. Some are smart, and some are dumb. Some have defects and others are perfect. My kind is the strongest, except for natural born; those are the Albinos, who are said to be the strongest of vampires. They are direct bloodlines of Dracula. It's a freak of nature, he doesn't have any way of making the Albinos, it just happens. He just finds them and gets them into his secret society. The second strongest are people like me; We are the one's who's been bitten directly by Dracula himself. There are only a few of us in the world. Anyone bitten by Dracula is considered royal blood. It only takes two days for the virus to change us. Usually our pigmentation changes over time, much like the Albinos, but we do keep a lot of our color and we can stand the sun much easier. Albinos must almost always stay away from anything that has the do with ultraviolet rays. Both Albinos and my kind are usually contortionist and extremely strong. It's very hard to kill us. I saw an Albino machine-gunned down and live. It takes my kind about two weeks to heal from major injury, but I've seen an Albino completely heal in just a week. The majority of the vampires are the weakest forms; those are the ones, like the two guys I bit; they are not bitten by Dracula directly. It takes about three to six weeks for the virus to affect them. They can heal fast, but usually they show scars. Sometimes these people can heal from the virus, but usually, if they remit, then they die."

The stewardess walks up, "What will you have today?" Sarah orders rare steak and red wine. The Stewardess reaches her tray and pours wine in a glass. She hands Roy two bottled waters and a white cloth, wrapped. He oddly looks, "Thanks." He holds the bottle up and begins to ask, "How did you know I wanted water?" Holding up the neatly folded cloth, "What's this?" "Oh, it's compliments from the pilot." She winks, and walks away. Roy sees the handkerchief around her neck; it's white, but has the same look of the clothes he found in the tomb. Roy chugs a bottle and unfolds the cloth; it's white and fluffy. It almost looks like pure white cotton candy and doesn't have an odor. He places his tongue on the white fluff; it taste sweet in his mouth. He begins eating on it; it's like eating a very light bread.

Sarah looks, "What's that?" "I don't know; that lady just gave it to me." She replies, "I've never seen anything like that, what's it taste like?" Roy responds, "It's sweet. Here, try some." Sarah tastes a small piece that melts on her tongue. She makes a face, "Yuck, it doesn't have any flavor at all; It's like eating snow or something." She becomes concerned, "You know, we've been on this plane for hours, and I've had to go to the restroom four times. Since we've got on the plane, all I've seen you do is drink, but I've never seen you go to the bathroom. No werewolf I know of could do that." Roy knows Sarah is catching on that he's no werewolf. He smirks, "And I'll tell you something else that's strange; I've not eaten in weeks; well, except for this bread stuff." Sarah blinks in surprise.

Roy looks up and focuses down the isle. He searches for the stewardess. At the end of the isle, a light flashes by. He looks at Sarah, "You know, maybe I should try and go to the bathroom now; I'll be back." He stands and makes his way to the front of the plane and goes down the stairs. Nothing. He feels the energy, but he doesn't see it. Returning up the stairs, he watches the stewardess step out of the cockpit entrance. He sees it, the white figure. Blocking his sight, she shuts the door behind her and approaches; "How did you like the bread?" It catches him off guard, "Oh, yeah, it was good." "Just good?" "Great, it actually tastes great." She smiles and walks past him, "I thought you'd like it." A question mark hits him as he stares at the cockpit entrance.

The stewardess glances back and notices Roy staring towards the cockpit "Is everything alright?" He turns, "Uh, yeah." He walks toward the woman and ask, "So, you said that the pilot gave me the bread?" "Yep." "Why?" "Well, you are our platinum flyer and you are from the service, right?" "That's right." She check marks the air, "There you go." She walks to the kitchen to get the hot meals. Roy's dumbfounded. He feels the same energy that he felt at the souvenir shop in Giza. Something's a foot; he just can't place his mind on it.

Roy returns to his seat. Sarah's eating the rare steak. He smells it, "It smells good, but I can't stand anything not cooked all the way, especially blood, it just stinks to me." He sits. She takes a sip of wine, "Hey, how come the stewardess didn't take your order?" Roy scrambles his memory, "She must have overheard me say I wasn't hungry."

Sarah goes blank, "I don't remember you saying you wasn't hungry?" Roy shrugs it off, "Awe, that's alright. I really am not hungry anyway." Sarah really enjoys her food. Roy notices that she doesn't eat the potatoes or snap peas. "Have a problem with vegetables?" She smiles while holding up a pierced piece of steak, "Meat eater." She bites the steak and savors it in her mouth. Roy watches her eat the food; he can almost taste it himself. He notices his energy, and feels a little perky; He thinks it's because of the bread he ate. "Wow, I feel great."

Sarah glances as she swallows, "Oh yeah, I almost forgot. Wine makes us extremely horny, we get buck wild when we have a bottle or more." Roy looks, "Anyone would get wild if they drank a bottle of wine." "No, not like vampires." She scans her mind as her brow flutters, "You know, I'm telling you all this stuff about vampires. Why don't you go and see for yourself. This Saturday, there's a show; you can go and see with your own eyes. That's the best way to learn about us." Roy's puzzled, "What show?" "The Cat Walk, it's a fashion show. We're always there. Every kind of vampire and canine you could possibly imagine will be there; you should go. It's really easy to get in; all you have to do is be a part and have the money. I have a number you can call for tickets."

The flight is long. Sarah flicks through the stations and begins to watch the news. Roy interrupts, "Hey, so what's your plans when you get to Texas?" She takes the headphones off and answers, "Oh, I don't know yet. I'll have to play it by ear, I guess." Roy keeps the conversation going until the news passes its coverage on Egypt. The commercial comes on. "Whew." A breath flows out of his mouth. Sarah never notices the television, but appears disturbed. Roy picks up her negative vibes. He thinks she may have just seen the coverage. Hardening her face, she speaks, "Oh yeah, I do have one more thing." A breath of relief goes out his nose, "What's that?" "There's one more vampire class. They're called the pack. It's some ancient agreement between vampires and the fallen one's; Well, you call them demons. I didn't believe in them, until yesterday, I saw them. They were horrible. These vampires are rumored to be even stronger than the werewolves, that's unless a werewolf is in the pack too." Roy interrupts, "Werewolves are stronger than vampires?"

Sarah lifts her eyebrows, "Yeah, but werewolves have the same strength of a third level vampire, that's until they change. When they change, then they are much stronger, but are like wild dogs. I've only heard of Dracula being able to keep them tame. Werewolves can kill vampires, but they are just like any dog to me. Demons are the only one's I know who can stop werewolves." Roy gets angry when she mentions demons. "What about normal people?" Sarah nods, "Well no, a person really has to be messed up in the head or they have to be very unsanitary or disturbed before a demon could go in; I really don't know the whole story of why demons don't go into humans, but it could have something to do with the pack. The bad news is that the demons can easily go in vampires and werewolves. It's legend that Dracula formed the pack between the demons and the vampires, the humans could just be another use for some greater cause; however, if you think about it, vampires are really human anyway; we could be the true goal of demons. The werewolves are the ones who get the bad end of the stick, because if they don't belong to Dracula, then the demons do what they want with them. If it wasn't for the pack, then I guess we'd all be screwed."

＊

Guardian of Man, Watcher of Spirits

The plane lands at the O'Hara Airport in Chicago. Sarah and Roy grab their bags to go inside and await their next flight. He tells Sarah to meet him at the coffee shop. He stalls; perhaps he will see the pilot. A voice of a man interrupts. "Sir, you will have to get off here." He turns; it's a man in uniform. Roy's disappointed, he's curious about his flight. "Yeah, okay." He steps off while glancing through the windowed walkway. She's met at the coffee shop. "Well Sarah, I guess this is the part where we say goodbye." She hands him the number, "This is where the Catwalk will be. Just call this number and mention my name, Tara will set you up." Roy takes the number. "Thanks." Her heart begins to beat hard. Everything around seems to revolve around him. It's the feeling a person gets during those last moments, those special times that one knows cannot be recaptured. She smiles and anticipates his speech. Roy counts the number of beats of her heart; He feels her pain. The warmth of her aura illuminates, the Gargoyle bask in her sun. Silence hits them both; it's that time. He reaches his hand out to shake hers; Sarah gives him the look of comfort and shakes his hand. She let's go, and drops her bag and tightly embraces him. Tears stream her eyes. "Thank you. I'll never forget you Roy; you're my savior." She kisses his cheek, pulls back, wipes her tears and smiles, "Goodbye." She lifts her bag, turns and walks off into the crowd; her spirit's found peace.

Roy walks to his flight and waits to get onboard. The flight attendant at the desk answers the phone. She pages, "Could a Roy Johnson please come to Terminal Twelve B?" Roy, standing in front of the lady responds, "That's me." She hands him the phone. "Hello?" There's quietness. He knows someone is there, "Who's this?" No answer. He doesn't hear any breathing, just the sound of a busy airport surrounding him. A woman's voice sounds, "What do you see in a kiss?" Roy's lost, "Huh?" The voice replies, "It's a pointless cause with no effectual meaning, is wasteful behavior." He figures, "Is this Sarah?" "No, this is not Sarah." "Well, it sure sounds like you." "Why of course I am me." "Sarah?"

The phone beeps; the flight attendant interrupts, "I'm sorry, but I am going to have to answer that." She presses the hold button and reaches for the receiver; He hands it over and waits. When she finishes the call, she speaks, "You're going to have to use the pay phone for personal calls Mr. Johnson; so, you might want to tell that person on the other end." Roy nods. She clicks the phone over and hands it to his anxious ear, "Hello?" He hears a dial tone. He looks at the hold buttons, there's no lines waiting. He glances up at the attendant and then presses star sixty-nine. The operator recording goes off, "…That option is not available from this phone, please hang up and try your call again." Roy hangs up; he ponders the outcome of the wayward vampire. Before he boards for home, an oddly shaped shadow captures his sight; it sets over a man, who eats popcorn. Its black eyes clicks up, catching Roy's stare. He knows it's a demon. His blood boils; all those people in Giza. Besides, he cannot stand their smell. Roy ignores the creature and boards the plane.

Touchdown, Roy's home. He rides the escalator down to the bottom level where wait's the taxi driver. He's amazed, the moving stairs held him up. A sign of relief hits his chest; this is one journey he'll never forget. "Click", the door opens to his new apartment, "Wow." Roy is pleased. As he tours, his smile lights the room. The toilet is made of steel, overlaid with marble, The Jacuzzi is lined with non slip rubber and surrounded by black swirled marble; The dining area has steel chairs overlaid with marble and brown leather padding. His king size bed's supported by steel, and sports a tiger skinned comforter and zebra pillowcases. The copper marbled floors and steel overlaid with marble furniture is a wonder to his brightened eyes; Blacksmith did an excellent job, the place looks like a kings palace.

Over the next few days, Roy studies the scrolls. With his cases of bottled water, he drinks and searches for matching ancient words, but finds nothing. He scans one of the scrolls and faxes it to an UCLA Historian Professor, who specializes in ancient hieroglyphics and writings; the efforts are wasted, the professor has no idea what the words mean. One of the scrolls features a giant sized lion with wings. Facing the lion is a woman, holding a sword. A light goes off in Roy's head; it's the flaming sword. The woman looks exactly like the beautiful winged creature he faced in Giza. He spends hours searching the internet for pictures of angels and demons, when at last, a finding. It's the lion-faced creature with wings.

The picture from the article is an exact match. The name under the picture is Abatton. He pulls up everything on the name and reads. Abatton's a high angel who is once said to be God himself. Abatton is portrayed as the one who holds the keys to hell. He's the one who binds Satan for a thousand years. Abatton's portrait is often seen standing between half human and half lion or half bird and half lion like creatures. On the other side of the half-human creatures, stands people, who sacrifices babies and animals to the half human like creatures. The half-human creatures look identical to many statues and drawings of the Sphinx.

One drawing features Abatton sitting on a throne, holding a tiny scepter in his right hand; It's the same long scepter Roy saw at the tomb. The scepter is used by Abatton to open a portal under the throne, where lays thousands of grotesque creatures, many of them resembling life sized grasshoppers. Roy speaks out, "Locust." It dawns on him, he remembers seeing the massive throne, were he used the seating of it to cover the hole over the underground tomb. The revelation grips him; Abatton was protecting something. He researches the name Kavin Drakon. His mouth drops, when he finds the meaning of the name. A great question overwhelms him, "Who is this Kavin Drakon, where did he come from?" The gargoyles quest continues.

Roy unfolds the dark clothes and stares. The mystery taunts him;

He's under the siege of his own imagination. Who is Abatton and who's Legion? "Legion." Roy darts to the computer and types the name Legion. The horror unfolds; Stories of countless people who are known to rip there own bodies, merge from the text of hundreds of articles. There's an ancient story of a man so strong, that he used his bare hands to kill a thousand armed roman soldiers. He dashes for the television and sees the reports, "…All across the country, terrorist strike as new shocking footage of thousands running through the streets in riots tearing their clothes off, killing, burning and setting themselves on fire." Roy follows the pattern. The footage starts from Egypt and crosses to the United States. His eyes light up, "It's Legion." He switches to the local news, "…A one man band sweeps across the U.S. He's robbed several stores and banks. He's seen here, in San Bernardino as he escapes from the high speed car chase which ends the lives of six innocent people who were waiting on the bus." The news astounds him. Roy desires to get out for a while, so he sets out on the town.

Dusk nears; a small child plays with a plastic bag, which seems to whirl in the wind. The child laughs as his mother who watches, giggles at the spinning child. Roy looks over the child and sees a man hovering over the child. He lands on the ground and sits. The child reaches for the bag as the man jumps up and spins the bag into the air. No one sees the man who wears a white cloak; it's the same material found in the tomb. Roy feels an incredible amount of energy from the child. Amused, the laughter and play entertains his mind. The mother looks up at Roy, who smiles and stares; she worries and takes her child inside. Warmth of peace overflows him, as he approaches the man who sets on the low stucco fencing. He gazes at his white hair, "Who are you?" "Apollos." "Are you an angel?" "I am Angelos, taster of joyous games, and you are Gargoyle of Arcangelos." The mans' eyes glimmer, "Arcangelos seeks you." Roy, confused, responds, "I'm Arcangelos." The man responds, "I know you are Arcangelos." "So, I am looking for myself?" The man smiles, "Something like that." Roy carefully sits down, "So how did you do that?" The man looks at him and repeats, "So how did I do what?" "How did you fly, you don't have wings." The man laughs, "Nothing you can't do, but with wings, you fly or without wings, you move." "What the hell did you just say?" "Not so smart, Gargoyle of Arcangelos, perhaps you stay grounded." Roy shakes his head, "Listen, I don't know you dude, but nothing you are saying makes sense. Why don't you show me how you did it instead of talking." The man stands, "Not so foolish, keeper of man, or shall I call you keeper of flames; She seeks you." "Kla-pow!" lightning hit's the dark cloud over head; the man is gone.

Roy walks towards the bus stop; gang members are mugging a man. He cries out as they kick him while taking his wallet and shoes. Roy stands and watches. The old lady looks at Roy, who's much bigger than the ruthless teens. He's captured in the moment, as the blood spews out the mouth of the man. The lady gets hostile with Roy, "Why don't you help him, you're bigger." The teens laugh and run off. The lady hitting him with her cane, "Why didn't you help him?" Roy smiles as he begins to walk off, "No demons here, those are just mad kids." A blank goes on her face as he walks past the injured man. Popping sounds of a knife slashing echoes into Roy's ears; it's a man being stabbed in his sleep.

Roy picks up the anger of the wife who caught her husband in the bed with another woman. The door flings open, as a half-naked woman rushes to her car and leaves. The raging yells of the wife gives him a rush, he's feeding off her emotions. The husband staggers out the door, his shirt drips of blood. Roy sees that the man was stabbed in his back and shoulder; He'll live. He hides behind the bush, awaiting her next move. As the man falls to the ground, she cries, "Why did you do it Carl, don't' you know I love you?" Roy suddenly burst out in a laugh. She turns in surprise of him watching. She stoops down and lifts, and helps her repentant husband back into the house.

Returning home, Roy's never had so much fun in his entire life. He sits in his chair and watches the news; Angels and demons pass through the screen. He's used to it. There's a connection between electricity and the angels. He first noticed it when he fought the creature in Giza, but now, he sees it up close and personal. He figures that the airwaves have something to do with demons and angels. "What's that?" He turns off the television. He hears it, the moans and grunts of two people having mad passionate sex. Under the soundproof floor, it's Starrlight, screaming out chants of excitement. Roy feels her pleasure, he tastes their lips as they kiss; He sees it clearly as if it was him with her. A new revelation is found, the angelic ears of the gargoyle experiences a vicarious occasion. After two hours, the beauty queen escorts a handsome blonde haired man to his yellow Lamborghini. The gate opens, the squealing tires burn the asphalt.

Morning renews; a new day is dawned. Roy returns from Blacksmiths shop, his leather sports a new pair of steel boots. He scans his schedule; it's almost time for the Catwalk. He tries on the tuxedo. The doorbell chimes; it's Starrlight. He opens the door to the frisky kitten, "Sugar plum, how are you?" She walks in, "Wow, this place is awesome!" Walking past him, she doesn't allow him a word. Her eyes bats, "I just love this place!" Roy follows behind the venturing diva. She turns and gives him a firm hand shake, "As you know, I'm Starrlight." Handing him her picture, she places it on his chest and signs it. "There you go; you can hang it in your bedroom." She steps to the door, "Well, it's been really nice to meet you, "Smooch." She kisses the air and walks out, but stops and turns, "Oh, I almost forgot. Michael came by; it's so sweet meeting basketball stars."

Roy scans his mind; he doesn't remember anyone named Michael who would know where he lives. "Okay, thanks." Turning as she twitches her tail, "Bye bye, sweetie, you're so sweet." The pussycat saunters away.

Roy walks to the garage, revealing his repaired corvette; He opens the door and reaches in, the engine starts. He feels the electricity in the air. He knows something's going on with his body. As he slowly gets in, he finds a sign of relief; the car holds him up. He figures it out; he's able to shift his weight when there's electrical current flowing near. His metallic blood reacts with gravity and the magnetic electrostatic atmosphere.

At the Kodak Theater, he steps out; the valet attendant takes his car. He walks the red carpet and enters the theater. Inside, the place is jammed pack with photographers, buyers, celebrities and fashion designers from around the world, Roy reads some of the flashy ads, "Versace, Dries Van Norten, Tommy Hilfiger, Christian Dior, Jonathan Saunders, Ya Ya, Gucci; Damn, everybody's here." Roy's able to hold his weight in his seat, he's getting used to this new method of defying gravity; it's the wiring and plugs under the carpet, they help him levitate. Looking around to see if anyone notices his movements, a smirk eases across his face; he's found a new toy.

The show begins. Across the runway, prances the most beautiful people man has ever seen; they're vampires. Their legs are eloquent; their skin is like silk. Both the men and women's walk, entrances, their physique is captivating. They dance the dance of exuberance as eyes melt at their will. Roy looks around in the audience, he's surrounded with people, there's vampires and canines everywhere, who bask in their pool of exotic entertainments. After the eye peeling show, there's an after party. The show gets heated up, as onlookers begin to ravish each other, seeking refuge to vent their lust under stage or in private quarters.

The after show features nudes and erotic pleasure unmentionable to virgin ears. The wine splashes the waves of lustful dainties, engulfing spirits to call their own. The vampires go wild; it's way too much for virgin eyes.

Across the wine toast, is the group of celebrities who's won countless Oscars. Roy spots Starrlight who sits next to Brad Bledsoe, President of ASCAP, the American Society of Composers, Authors, and Publishers. He walks by as she notices and grabs his arm, "Hey honey, Michael came by again, you guys have so much in common. You should go out sometime."

Roy looks edgy, "There's no guy named Michael around here that knows me and I sure the hell ain't gay, I like girls." Starrlight giggles, "Who said anything about a guy, Michaels a girl honey, and she's pretty and nice, she's really tall, but you know more about those athletes than I do. I don't watch the WNBA, but I know I saw her on television. maybe she's got a crush on you or something, you guys should give it a try, she's really sweet, you'll like her." He begins to argue, when a low grumbling in his ear catches his attention. Roy senses demons and rushes out. It's a black SUV spinning off into the night. His blood curdles; he rushes the parking tenant to get his car. When the tenant brings the car around, Roy pulls him out, while throwing a hundred dollar bill out the window. He spins around the corner, he looks for the SUV; something about it smells bad.

Three hours, Roy pulls up, opposite side of the Foxes Tail Lounge. He spots the SUV. Out steps three vampire demons and four women who walk inside. This is the second time he's encountered demon-possessed vampires. He smells them, and counts the odors; there's hundreds of them, drinking blood of innocent victims from the Catwalk. He doesn't care about vampires, but something about these vampires rubs him the wrong way. He recollects and speaks under his breath, "Not yet." and peels off, breezing through the blood infested air. Nearing home, the corvette spins around the corner. Roy sees the dark aura emitting from Starrlight's room. He slams his breaks and jumps out; something's amiss.

Her voice is heard through a muffled mouth, she's being raped. Over the gate flies the gargoyle. He smells the stench brimstone.

Inside, Starrlight struggles as the stranger reaches his point. With his hand over her mouth, he pushes her head to the side into the mattress, revealing her jugular. Just as he breaks her skin, "swoop!" He flies backward into the brick wall cracking it at impact. The dust hits his head as he jumps up and yells, "Gargoyle!" Roy's eyes light up, it's Brad Bledsoe. He throws several fast punches at Roy's mid section and face, but is blocked on every twist and turn. Roy's surprised; the vampire's extremely fast and strong. Bledsoe curses, "Fuck you!" and dashes down the hall into the foyer where he kicks the hinges off the front door, making his exit. Before Bledsoe makes the corner, Roy pounces him. They roll as Bledsoe springs up. Bledsoe kicks and sends Roy flying into the bushes. He stands, "It's you, Legion!" He spits and jackals onto an oncoming car; Legions out of sight.

Roy feels that he could catch the car, but changes his mind on his pursuit. As he returns, he looks at the door. "Thank God the Gonzales's took the old lady in the upper apartment over their mothers this weekend." Roy peeks into the door at the curled up movie star. "I better call the cops." Through tears, "No, no don't, you can't do that." "This mother fucker just raped you, are you kidding me?" "I'll be alright. I don't want this to get out to the news." He hangs up his cell phone. "No, you're not alright."

Roy bends down and holds out his hand. Wrapped in the sheet, she turns and embraces him, letting out uncontrolled whimpers, "I don't believe it! Who would believe that the head of ASCAP raped me? Out of all the people in the world, it had to be my best friend." Roy looks at her neck, "Whew." no cuts. He carries the shocked Barbie doll up to his apartment. "You can stay here. Do you want me to call anyone?" "No, please don't, please don't, I don't want anyone to know about this, okay?" Roy doesn't like her idea, but agrees, "Okay." His cell goes off, "Mr. Johnson, the doors busted." It's the security guard. "Oh yeah, Clarence, we're working on the door, you can have the night off." "Are you sure?" "Yeah, everybody's gone anyway and I'm having the front redone in the morning anyway." "Okay, Mr. Johnson, if you need anything, just give me a call." "Alright Clarence." The phone hangs up, as the voice of a happy guard leaves the gate and drives off. She looks at him, "Thanks for sending him away. I don't want anyone to know about it." Roy nods. Starrlight rambles on for four hours straight. It's amazing how people act when they experience trauma. She talks it out; after seven cups of coffee and a few trips to the bathroom, she unwinds through the talk of how her mother got trapped in the bathroom on the airplane. A snoring sound is heard through blonde hair tucked into her knees. Roy picks her up, lays her on his bed, and tucks in her broken spirit. He shuts the door and goes into the living room. He leaves a message for Blacksmith to make that steel door he was talking about, "Oh yeah, and make the knocker into a gargoyle, maybe a lions face and half man or something…Okay call me when you get this message." He hangs up. It's research time. The long hours into the morning and Roy finds little to nothing on gargoyles. All he knows is that there's a strong relation to water and gargoyles. Denial sets, he thinks it's all myth.

Roy knows why the vampire was there; He feels he's being watched. He thinks about Sarah and Starrlight, the innocent people; all because of Dracula and his side kick Legion, so many die. There's no mistake, something brews inside him; it's anger. He mumbles, "On Monday, I'm putting an end to this."

Los Angeles is at rest, no roses sold, no horns blown by the mid shift traffic. The birds sing, the flowers sway, even the dust lay. Families gather for feast and fellowship, lost souls find rest in chapels; The wino sets his bottle aside and looks up; The hot sun steams away the morning dew, it's Sunday.

Blacksmith finishes, the steel door displays the new gargoyle-knocker and chime. After gathering his stuff, Blacksmith begins to pull off. Roy speaks, "Thanks for coming; I owe you for taking your day off from church service." Blacksmith smiles, "No problem, I always have time for family. If anything else comes up, just let me know." Roy grins, "Alright man, see you later." He presses the remote, allowing the truck to leave. He waves goodbye to a shook up Starrlight, she's on her way to New York; she's doing a shoot tomorrow, Never Bend a Buck Two. The limousine eases off into the daystar of entertainment. His smile goes serious, turning, he marches up to his apartment. When he goes in, he notices, "Somebody's been in here." He looks around, the television remotes moved, it was on the counter, but now it's on the television. He scans the room, no smell; it wasn't a demon.

His picture's been turned, it once faced the wall, but now it faces the window. "I've never moved this." He feels the eyes watching; He rushes to the hall as a ghostly figure dissipates into the blistering sun. Roy gets frustrated, it's his first time not being able to figure things out, "This shits going to end soon."

Roy ponders, he's thinking about his options. There could be way too many vampires; he needs a back up plan. He studies one of the scrolls, it shows a gargoyle hanging upside down from the temple, it appears to be watching a demon, which stands underneath. He takes off his boots and concentrates; jumping up, he lands on his butt. Dusting himself off, Roy goes again, "Thump!" The floor punches the back of his head. Again, "Clack!" He opens his eyes, the ceilings under his feet. He hangs and squats like a frog as he looks down at the floor. Upside down, he studies the scrolls; it's the angel with the sword.

Roy jumps down and walks to the safe hidden in his floor. The black vault opens; it's the flaming sword setting in the gun case. He pulls it out and unwraps the black cloth. The cloth's identical to the material he found in Giza. Taking a deep breath, he grabs the handle and holds it. Nothing; The handle feels cool in his hand. Without removing the sword from the sheath, he picks it up. It feels light in his hand, so natural, as if the sword could speak, saying that it was made just for him. He showers; it's time to suit up. As he slips it on, the black material feels cool. After he pulls on the top and bottom pieces, he lassos the sword around his waist. With a two-gallon jug of purified water on his side and the heavy black hooded robe in his lap, Roy sits in the center of his living room floor and waits; He's ready for war.

* * *

Battle of Angels

Skip walks to the entrance, "He's with me." John follows in behind. In the Casino, Connie looks over at the crap table; it's a signal for Skip to walk over there. Behind the crap table sits Xan Bledsoe. He stands and ignores Skip, "Have a seat John." "No, I'd rather stand." "Suit yourself." Skip interrupts, "Hey, I told you I could find him." Xan never likes to be over talked, "Table sixty nine needs drinks, why don't you go and help the girls." Skip frowns, "But that's all the way through to the diner." Xan smirks, "But of course it is." Skip knows he better start moving, "See you later-on John."

Xan looks, "You've shown yourself to be quite a remarkable candidate. I've one more task, and you will not only be a part, but I have ambitions for you to head my groupies. They need a leader, someone of ultimate intelligence, and John, your genius has proven just that. It seems that my brother has taken a fall and, well, one day, he will be replaced. I will most definitely fill his shoes, but as I ponder that thought, I must find someone who wears a size ten in Foxes Deluxe Leather." Xan looks down at the twenty five thousand dollar boots John earned when he hacked into a Swiss bank account.

Johns disappointed that he's not made it into the secret society of the Goths. "That's just bullshit!" Xan's impressed at the boldness of John, "Yes, more hate, love to see it in your eyes; let's take a walk." Xan walks along side an angered gothic. "You know what I like about you John, you and I have so much in common. My mother and father hated me just like yours hated you. From foster home to foster home, no one wanted us. The students think you're a freak, they don't understand your ways; the way you dress, the way you wear your hair, your tattoos, your body piercing. No one respects your intelligence, you're a misfit, an outcast. I can relate to all those things; for years and years, I spent my life stuck in a cruel world. A world that underestimated my prowess. It's hard for people to accept a genius, and likewise, it's hard for the genius to accept foolish people. Just like you, I was an outcast, but I didn't allow that to hinder me from being the most powerful man in the world."

John stops in his tracks, "Hey, save the tear jerker crap, just tell me my next job so I can get this shit over and done." Xan drops his smile as they stare each other down. Evil settles, Xan puts his arm around Johns shoulder, and walks him towards the restaurant. "That's what I like about you John; you're straight to the point." They approach table one. Xan sits and holds out his arm, "Have a seat." John remains standing. Xan, knowing Johns frustration, reaches into his suit. It's a beige folded cloth. "Here." He hands it to John who reaches, "What's this?" "It's insurance." John unfolds the cloth, revealing words translated from Greek into English, written in blood." John knows this paper's important. He slowly eases into the booth, opposite side. Xan takes a sip of wine, "Tell me what pisses you off more than anything in the world." John stares at the cloth and looks up, his eyes grows dark, "Certain people." Xan sets the wine down, "Exactly; they fucking piss you off!" Xan looks up at Kendall who leans over and opens a dark burgundy case, housing two black twenty-two semiautomatic machine guns.

Xan's eyes lights up, "It's lunch time and schools out." John knows what Xan wants, to execute the students that made fun of him in school. John pulls off his trench coat and straps the double leather holder. He places the trench coat back on, and takes the guns and places them in the holsters underneath. Xan sits back and motions, Kendall walks away. He looks into the face of the kid who stares at the words, and just as he

114

starts to read them, "No, don't read it just yet." John looks up, "Why not?" "Those words are sacred; they are the very words I spoke before I became who I am. It's a summons." "A summons?" Xan points at the words, "This is what you say when things just don't go as planned. It can only work when your heart's full of anger. That's when you will know his true power; Lucifer's magnificence becomes one!" "How do I know when the time is right?" Xan smirks, "You will know." He orders John a steak. "We are expecting a guess tonight and I want you to hang around. Just in case things don't go as planned, I want you to use this." He folds the cloth up and places it inside Johns' coat. John gets the sense that something important is going to take place tonight, so he sits back, watches the guest and hangs around. Xan leaves, he has a meeting with Dracula. Connie meets him at the elevator, "So, does your apprentice knows what he's getting into?" "Who cares, just as long as our goals are met." Xan avoided telling John the full truth; the etched words summons Legion instead of Satan.

The black limo sits, three stalkers emerge. Roy smells them, they're only vampire; It's party time. Placing on the hooded robe, He walks out the entrance and sets his eyes on the target. "Swoop." His feet softly lands on the other side of the gate, the vampire's laugh. The muscle guy mocks, "Here kitty kitty." "Zoom." His feet fly into the air and land his face, sending the sunglasses into oblivion. The other takes a swing, but before he lands, he's on his back, holding his stomach. Roy reaches into the drivers' side, and just as he begins to snatch the shirt through the window, a voice yells out, "No, I'm just a girl!" He peers in, "I see, you are." "I'm just doing my job, they told us to pick you up." The two vampires stand, they're in pain. Roy sees her aura, she's only human, and tells the truth. "They are expecting you for dinner." "I've been down this road before." He gets in and looks out the window at the two scuffed men, "You'll be walking back." He nods to her, the limo starts up, the two are left behind to taste the night air. As the limo pulls off, his face goes angry, he warns them, "And walk real slow." The limo pulls up; it's the Foxes Tail Lounge. Roy steps out, fire's in his eyes. As the driver pulls away, his robe rustles in the breeze; a storm's coming.

The phone rings, Dracula picks up, "Yes." It's Legion. "I delivered you the gargoyle, now's my turn, Drakon! "Click." Dracula pauses, then hangs up the receiver. Connie looks up with question. Xan speaks, "Who was it? "Your brother, he's on his way." Xan cringes, "Damn him, if he hurts my brother." Dracula speaks, "And what?" "Do you think you're a match? He'll rip you into shreds." Xan expresses his feelings, "I gave him my strongest man, he has the cunning of the greatest, even Hitler." Dracula refers to John, "The goods are not delivered yet!" Xan, frustrated, "The kid is upstairs as we speak. When Legion gets here, I will deliver John personally."

Dracula interjects, "If not, then my pure breeds will handle Legion as they did before." She resists, "What if they turn against you?" Dracula smacks her face, sending Connie across the floor. "She stands and wipes the blood from her mouth. "Smack!" Her legs buckle as she lands on her butt. Dracula stands over her, "You get up when I tell you to get up!"

Connie keeps her head down, facing the floor. She knows she's out of line; she's the only one who ever gets away with saying anything without being killed.

Roy walks under the canopy, Kendall, Jerrod and Damon stands along side the host who's seating guest. Roy breaks the line and goes in front facing an angry-nervous Kendall. Roy stops and gives Kendall the eye, "How's the nuts?" Kendall doesn't like what he just heard, as Roy walks through, causing Kendall to step back, allowing Roy to pass. No one follows behind while he walks through the luxurious feast. It's celebrity night; Familiar faces, members of ASCAP and the Screen Actors Guild glamour's the Hollywood hustle; their kissing each others ass. Roy humors himself as he looks through the illustrious sea of faces, "Must be rump roast night."

The wandering eyes of canines and vampires watch, as the passer-by is untouched or questioned; the doors open, he enters the casino. The half-nudes don't phase his eyes, which are set for the elevator down the hall. At the elevator, the topless host nervously keys the hole, allowing Roy to enter alone. Her scared smile is held back as the door closes, separating the two; He's going down.

Kendall walks to the elevator and radios his earpiece. "The gargoyle is set." Xan responds, "Let's see if he's able to figure it out, let him through, but don't show him the way." The door opens, Roy steps out and ventures through the underground stores.

Roy walks into the winery, the merchant looks-on as the gargoyle steps into the back, where aging wines are stored in wood casings. The hairs on his neck raises, he feels their presence, but doesn't see them. "I know you're here." Roy stops and stands. In the middle of the floor, lays a pentagram the size of an airplane hangers gateway. He notices the line down the center; it reminds him of the old bomb shelters. "Looks like two tanks could drive through." It dawns on him; it's an underground entrance. There's no hinges, no locks or handles. His blood boils; he turns and spots an outlet, the plugs casing goes underground. He places his ear to the plug, he feels the electricity; something's down there. Staring at the outlet, Roy stands and paces back; He's going for it. "Ka-Bam!" a bolt of lightning enters through the socket.

Dracula's lair, the unseen city. A flash of lightning hit's the ground, Roy stands, his clothes and swords still intact. The unseen world, shadow of the upper city. Roy reads the dimly lit street sign, "City of Lost Angels." His eyes pop out; it's surrounded by two city blocks of civilization. It almost looks like down town Los Angeles, with a church as the city's center; it's a castle. The stench of blood and brimstone reeks the land. Roy knows that this is where the blood supplies are brought. The city inhabits ten thousand city dwellers, all of them vampires and werewolves possessed by demons; they're the pure breeds.

Growling sounds hisses the air, red and black eyes watches from the dark, as a ready gargoyle approaches the castles entrance. At the entrance, is a drawbridge lowered, Roy crosses. Two twelve foot griffins' stands, facing; they almost look real. Roy touches one of them; "Petrified." Life once breathed through their nostrils; the surreal grips his throat, he feels natures call.

Roy raises his hands and pushes in the two pentagram handles, the double doors open. As the massive doors swing, the wind catches his robe and flaps it in the dust. Dracula stands at the bottom of the winding staircase. He's wearing the same clothing Roy wears. "I'm glad you're here; Want you join us for dinner?" Dracula holds his hand out, pointing towards a large hallway, which leads to the kings dining hall.

Dracula leads, as Roy follows into the dining cathedral. A large round table centers twelve ancient seats, six on either side of the throne of black marble; each seat is padded with red leather and laced with gold and precious stones and rubies. Waiting, is a feast, rare steak and every kind of grape and berry; Large cherry-wood goblets are set, where centers a crystal fountain, trickling red wine into the birdbath of eloquence.

The four female vampiress dressed in see through silk gowns bow their heads and leave the two to feast. The king of vampires speaks, "Let's eat." Dracula points to the furthest seat from the throne "Have a seat." Roy hesitates. Dracula insists, "Please?" Roy sits, his outer robe moves to the side, revealing the sword. Dracula notices, "Oh, I see we've been shopping the same clothing store; Nice tailor, don't you think?" Roy doesn't answer. "You know, this clothing is far advanced for this world. Non friction, and yet, able to bend light; Now that's true technology."

Dracula takes his seat on the throne. Throwing his head back, he speaks, "Nice blade, too bad you can't use it, and yet, it is remarkable how you carry such a delicate instrument. I had wondered how the angels were able to successfully retrieve it out of my shop, without breaking the bearers code, but now it all comes to mind, why of course, use the gargoyle. No gargoyles been able to do this in past attempts, as the blade would destroy them. Even the strongest of demons have attempted to master such array, but all have failed; and yet, you, you have it. Truly, you must be the strongest of them all. Why did you wait so long to retrieve it? Perhaps you were afraid of the fate of your former kind. You do know how it all came to pass don't you?" Roy glances down at the blade, "No, tell me Kavin Drakon." Dracula's impressed. "I've not been called by that name in such a long time. How come we're just meeting for the first time? Perhaps the angels had a plan to stop my peril." Roy smirks, "That's not your real name." "Oh yeah, then what may I ask is my real name?" Roy smirk drops into an angry frown, "Kain." Dracula stands, "Fuck you, hoarder of mans' emotions!" in rage Dracula begins, "Was it not your kind who started this madness? You walk around with your pious inventions, seeping up every ounce of mans will, while you bask in their ignorance. It's because of you, that I bear this name!"

Dracula looks into Roy's eyes; He sees the uncertainty. "You look as lost as they come, Roy, or shall I call you Gargoyle, keeper of the way. It all makes sense to me now; for over two thousand years, I've been searching for you, but they hid you right under my nose; Right here. While I was destroying your city, you were making plans on attacking me at home; a brilliant plan. Legion had mocked me for eons, he said that you were dead and were nonexistent; that was until you two encountered in Giza. Poor poor Sarah; What ever become of her. The rumors came to me that you broke the code of bearers and extracted the sword. Therefore, I sent Legion in to see if the sword was gone. The horror, it brought fear in the hearts of every demon, even Legion shook his boots. Therefore, they turn to me, and do you know why? Because I don't fear you. To me, you don't exist; you're dead."

Dracula throws his hands up, as he turns, "But, I am certain you feel the same way about me. So, why the question mark, why do you look so unsure?" He gazes at the sword around Roy's waist. I am certain that you were not there, how they hid you from me, well, that remains a mystery that you will take to your grave."

Roy's curiosity sparks, "What did they hide from me?" "Your origin. It's the same method they use to keep all creatures under control. Take away a person's origin and you take his power. So, you want to know about the sword?" "Yes." "Well, I don't know what they've told you, but this is the full story." The room grows cold, Roy knows that he's about to be taken on a mind trip.

Dracula paces around the table, stops and gives Roy a long stare; His eyes flare as he speaks, "To know about the sword, one must know how it all began." He paces around, "If heaven was so perfect, then why was there war there? The city above the clouds, cloaked from the eyes of they who believed, hidden from the minds of those who reasoned. No one knows exactly how they became our leaders and soon to be the decision makers of our very existence, but there was a place called the holies where abode the very essence of God himself; that's if it ever existed. However, that's not important; what is important is who's responsible for the mess we struggle in on a daily basis. Those persons are the real catalyst of all our misery and woe. There are five sources of intelligence, God, Seraphim's, Cherubim's, Angels and Humans. The Seraphim, being the highest are not able to tell us where they come from, or how long they've existed, but what they do know is that they're existence has a strong connection to the place they call the throne, the holies, where it is rumored that all things come from. The Seraphim are giant ancient creatures, all of them with six wings, the lion, the lamb, the eagle, the unicorn, the bull, the locust and dragon. These all lived in the arc, where abode the very essence of God. They were said to become pure energy when they entered the throne, but when they came out, they were massive, it was said that the lamb once sat on the sun and placed his foot on the earth. Outside were the Cherubim, Lucifer, Michael, Gabriel, and

Gaia. And the dwellers of the city were the angels. They are the children of Cherubim; I call them sons of God. It was in the city were all hell broke loose. Lucifer and Gaia were the first two to discover the genetic code, but it was the angels who took the idea and ran with it." Roy questions, "What idea?" "The creation of humans. It was the Cherubim who created the first humans; they were made by using DNA structures from the lower angels. The goal was to create the perfect human. There was great celebration at the birth of the humanoid, the creatures that resembled angels."

Dracula hardens his face, "There was one slight problem; it was the energy. The humans gave the angels something they'd never experienced, sexual drive. The humans were able to mate and regenerate, but it was the angels' telepathic abilities, they were able to feel what humans felt just from being in their presence. It was that energy which brought about a new thirst; it fed their minds and drove their desires. It was Lucifer who convinced the first angels that they could breed with humans, enjoy sex as humans do. The angels became more than desirous; they were infatuated with the beauty of the woman. A secret society was formed, to breed a new race of humans. These were the giants, Goliath, Ra, Ramses, the Olympians, Hercules, Sampson, Perseus and many more; they were like gods."

Dracula continues, "The Lamb was against these genetic ideas, He said that the Cherub and Angels along with their children were not ready for such inventions; He was right! Being able to survive off another's imaginings is extraordinary power; but just like all powers, too much of anything gets out of control; it can destroy you. During this exact timing, Gaia, against the elders counsel, began to combine human DNA with her own. This lead to the birth of the Gorgons; that's where I come into the picture. My biological mother, God rest her soul; it was she who told me of the many treasures of the land and of the Gorgons; a woman who was created so beautiful that even the higher angels desired her. I was entranced; I had to see for myself. My father warned me not to go, but, just as they say, curiosity kills the cat. And there it was, the treasures of the land. I gathered all I could, so that I could please the Lamb. But just as I would leave, Medusa tried to enchant me to face her, but I ran like hell; I wasn't fast enough. Before I could reach the sea, she bit me. Her venom would have killed me had it not been for the salt of the sea. I couldn't see, I was in pain; I should have died."

Dracula's eyes darken, "When the Lamb came into the garden, he knew right away that I was changed. The bastard would never accept anything I presented. But I soon figured it out. He could not feed off my emotions, because I was the half-breed of a higher angel. I was part human and part Gorgon. The venom drove me mad; my teeth grew, my skin became pale, I could not stay in the sun long, and most of all, I was tired of eating fruit; I became thirsty. It was that evening, when my brother Abel basked in the sun of his pleasure, that I bit him, I sucked every ounce of his blood until he was lifeless; just like the fruit from the ground, I buried him."

Dracula's voice deepens, "From that day, it was the Lamb who outlawed genetic engineering. This sent Lucifer into a rage. He formed the Legion of Angels, a new council against the government of heaven. It was then, that the battle of angels began. The angels would freely have sex with women; it was illegal for angels to mate with humans anymore."

A devious smirk smudges Dracula's face, "The minds of humans were the battlegrounds. It is an understatement, that we are merely pawns in the game; Humans are slaves. It was my race who broke the chain of events. Because of our unethical imaginations, the angels could no longer feed. From there, came the battle of angels. Lucifer fought against the Lamb; He was no match against the power of the mighty Seraphim. When the Legion of Angels destroyed their original heavenly bodies, their spirits sought refuge in humans. With the space of five minutes, they can enter into most living organisms; Dogs, cats, pigs, dolphins, humans and various creatures are they're prey. When they possessed our minds, they lost their way and begin to loose self-control; they burned within their own lust, killing themselves. It was the one DNA structure, which Lucifer underestimated, the desire to be free. Humans resisted order, thus, becoming the leaders of their own fate. Demons against demons, man against demons; the earth was corrupt. Many demons could not agree on any one subject. Lucifer concluded that human mind is far too weak to control. He sought other methods to control humans; thus, the pack was formed between the dark angels and my race. The elders could feed no more."

Dracula exuberantly expires, "Our plan was full proof, that is, until the Seraphim Judah mated with lower angels, forming the Lions of Judah. It was the Lions of Judah, who marched the earth. It was they, who taught the humans how to fight the demons and vampires. When it seemed that the humans were safe to fend on their own, then the Lions of Judah would soon return to heaven, but not without a token of safe keep."

Dracula disdains, "Since they were part lower angels, the Lions of Judah were able to mate with humans, forming a new race that would protect the humans from a world headed by Lucifer and Gaia. They were the Gargoyles. Half human, half lion. One of the greatest of ancients was a Gargoyle by the name of Sphinx of Judah. The idea caught on; soon, many heavenly creatures would crossbreed, forming a new gargoyle."

Dracula grotesquely tones, "The Gargoyles would protect humans from the demons in exchange for worship and treasure. It was the Gargoyles who helped stunted the growth of my race. I had a city, a great city of power, Sodom. The demons and vampires ruled the ancient city. Freedom to choose, freedom of will, Men loved whatever and whomever they wanted. This brought jealousy in the heart of the angels who convinced Michael and Gabriel to set ranks against me. It was Michael and Gabriel who took the head of Medusa and destroyed everything I created. It was at Sodom and Gomorrah, that all of my children died. From that day, I swore to take vengeance."

A fire glimmers Dracula's eyes, "After three days, heaven awaited the return of Michael and Gabriel, but not without certain peril; we ambushed them. Lucifer and Legion attacked from the front and I attacked the rear. Before the Gargoyles could assist, I took Medusas head and destroyed them. That night, every demon, every human, and every lower angel died at the power of the Gorgons head. Legion, the thousand half-breeds of Lucifer ran ramped, celebrating the death of Gargoyle. Everywhere that there were a Gargoyle, Legion would lead me to them; it was so easy. Michael, with her sword of flames retrieved the hideous head and hid it in the Sphinx. It's taken me thousands of years to find it. It was at the Sphinx where I saw Michael. I knew of her fascination of monuments, so I built one in her dedication. She fell for it, and entered the sanctuary. When an Archangel crosses the human path and dividing them is a heavenly object, then the family and their descendants obtain the right of bearer. It was there, where I marked the Sphinx with the scripts. By the time she realized it, it was too late; she had to leave the Sword of flames. For thousands of years, Michael wore the name of shame, the angel who lost the sword of God. This was another victory; Lucifer knew that it would be hard for her to defeat his army without the flaming sword."

The awakening experience grips Roy by the throat; it's hard to swallow. The revelations clear, he looks at his wrist where Michaels' wings cut him; it was her blood, which crossed his. The flaming sword sealed the metallic substance, leaving a mark on his wrist; it's his birthmark.

Dracula begins to defame, "I see you haven't touched your steak, your kind never does. I guess your stomachs not made for the better things in life. It must be torture not being able to eat. Instead, you feed on the souls of the ignorant. It's no wonder that you are extinct. Water bearers, that's all your kind are good for. I can't stand the sight of you, so arrogant in your wits. It is your fate; like all the others, you will taste the salt of your own bowels." Roy shows emotion, "You sick mother fucker. I don't care about you, your momma or your bullshit fairytales. As far as I am concerned, you can kiss my black ass!" The room grows silent, the nemesis is awake; Gargoyle lives.

＊

Gargoyle versus Dracula

The smell of brimstone engulfs the room, Connie and Xan steps in. Down the winding stairs, the growling sounds of hundreds of werewolves run into the dining hall, they await the command of Dracula. "Today is a day that will go down in history as the first Gargoyle to taste blood." Dracula takes his seat at the throne. He snaps his fingers "Roar!" the werewolves' growl at the Gargoyle. Roy stands and yells, "Sit down!" the werewolves, whimpering, heels. Again, Dracula snaps, the werewolves lay there heads down; the demons have lost control of the canines. Disgusted, Dracula speaks, "That's just it, never send a dog to do a mans business." He motions. Connie and Xan, dressed in all black leather, go into karate stance.

Dracula takes a bite of his bloody steak, sips his wine and slaps it down on the table. "Kick his ass!" Roy, an expert in martial arts is amused. Connie jumps; her kick is blocked. Xan goes for his back, Roy dodges, causing Xan to kick Connie's stomach. Several blows thrown simultaneously by the assailants are thwarted by the zipping speed of the Gargoyle. As Xan delivers several whipping kicks, Connie jumps

Roy's back and bites his neck. He grabs her hair, flipping her into the attacking vampire. They leap to their feet and assume another stance. Roy shakes his head, "You've got to be joking me." Connie yells, "Ahhh!" "Bam!" Roy kicks, her body catapults through the large oak door. Xan's foot lands Roy's midsection, as he catches it and twist, "Snap!" his thigh bones pop through his leg. He pushes Xan down. He tries to stand, "Floop!" Xan's neck pops back; it breaks as the lifeless vampire flops.

Dracula stands, "You haven't begun to touch me!" The smell gets stronger as all around him, swarms of Albino vampire demons attack. Roy moves like a wild cat, his feet flies into the air, leveling several. After the first hundred, more come. Roy's stuck in a sea of raging demons, the snaps of necks and backs sound the hall; there's too many of them. Hundreds of wild demonized fangs overturn the incredible strength and speed of the Gargoyle. Covered under thousands, the under world goes for his juggler.

Dracula looks on, as hundreds upon hundreds fly lifeless from the mountain of vengeance. Suddenly, screeching is heard as hoards of vampires run from the dark blue flame; Roy holds the sword. In one swooping action, thousands burn, killing both demon and vampire. The voice of Dracula echoes the halls, "Nooo!" He reaches into the seat of his throne and pulls out the blackened, slimy, worm eaten, snake infested Gorgon. The stench of death chokes the hall; It's the head of Medusa. The flame of the sword is overtaken as the black light burns through the halls, singeing flesh and bones, the crackling sounds roast the living. The fire torches out the castles openings, burning the under city. The screams of ten thousand demon vampires and werewolves are muffled under the rushing wind of the skull. Fire and brimstone beams out its eyes, the wake is death. Rotten smell of burnt blood and sulfur smolders the land; only two remain. The metallic blue veil covering Roy's eyes lifts, the terror is over.

With his arm stretched out, Dracula holds the head. The look of surprise eats his soul while his mouth hangs open; Roy's still alive. Roy levels the sword and slides it into its sheath. His hands are steady, not one burn marks his body. White mounds of molted salt separates the two. Roy looks through the heaps as their eyes meet, "Your turn bitch!" He leaps onto the ceiling, his feet cracks the enormous dome as he runs across and lands on the round table, leveling it to the ground. Ashes fly into the air; The Gargoyle taste blood.

Dracula lays the head in the seat, as he begins to speak, "Boom!" he flies through the wall into the library of Draconus. The eleven-foot case smashes him. Dracula pushes it off, but is snatched into the air; the Gargoyle strikes. Before Dracula can get a punch in, Roy lands his jaw, snapping it out of joint. "Thump, thump, thump!" Dracula's left eye is full of blood. "Crack!" his necks broken; the fight's over.

Roy rises up, the Overlord lays lifeless. As he looks around, the sea of death is appalling; this Dracula has caused much harm. "Pop." the neck of Dracula resets. Roy turns. Dracula stands. "Try that again Gargoyle." The shit hit's the fan; Dracula should be dead. The fire of rage embedded within Roy's heart, explodes. Sudden burst of lightning projects from his hands, landing Dracula's torso; Roy beats him senseless. "Bam, Bam, Bam, Bam!" Like a rag doll, his head tosses from side to side. "Die mother fucker, die!" Blood squirts across the downed bookcase, the vampire mocks.

Roy stops, the face of Dracula heals. "Aaah!" Dracula grabs him by the neck as they both lock the grip of death. Roy's too strong as he maneuvers underneath Dracula; bending him backwards over his chest, Roy tightens his chokehold. The hands of Dracula reaches, only to grab the lifeless air. Roy's eyes sparkle; he uses his power. His eyes fix on the sliver of a busted mantle piece, revealing his reflection. He stares, his arms wraps around the helpless master; Roy faces himself. His grip weakens, he's proved his point; Dracula's defeated. He pushes him off and rustles to his feet. Looking down at his awkward smirk, Roy speaks, "As far as I am concerned, you're already dead, Kain." The Gargoyle sets his face to the upper city; His business is done. The brick and mortar shuffles, Dracula holds up the head of Medusa, "I will destroy your world with it." Roy turns; he knows Dracula cannot accept his lost. As he goes for the sword, the wall explodes, "Roooar!" Roy covers his ears; the pain is immense. The ground quakes, the structure gives, wings push the walls and beams aside.

Dracula falls back, the shock holds him captive, the sight is too much. Roy calls, "Abatton!" The wings flutter, blowing him too his knees as he muffles his ears. The face of the lion closes, its nostrils the size of two houses. Dracula, full of terror, loosens his grip, the head falls from his hand. Abatton scoops the head with his fingernail. The paws of the giant closes, Medusa's returned. The six wings move rapidly, they appear transparent. The sound of a hundred ocean waves thunders the under city, "Ka-Bam!" Abatton's gone. Roy shakes his head, as he walks away; the viper has lost his sting. At the exit of Abatton, the lightning causes the Foxes Tail Lounge to shake; it's a small tremor. John looks around, two hours has past. He's never waited more than thirty minutes before. John becomes furious; he feels that he's being rejected. "This is bullshit!" He pulls out the cloth and speaks the words.

The door flies open, It's Brad Bledsoe. "We had a deal, where are you Drakon?" He stops in front of table one where sits John. He smiles, "I know what you want kid!" He pulls out a thirty-eight revolver and pulls, "Boom!" He drops. The people scream. They've just witnessed the head of ASCAP kill himself. John knows something's gone wrong. He looks around and rushes out before the cops come. Roy walks into the restaurant and spots Bledsoe. He counts the slow beats, the heart ceases; Legion lifts.

Roy cleans his watch, and speaks, "Five minutes, just five minutes." As he runs outside, the ambulance pulls up; people step aside. He looks around and traces the direction of the shadows, which follows the kid across the street. The sky thunder, blackness is in the air; there's a storm coming.

❋

The Kiss of Life

John looks over, "You've lost your rocks bro. You mean to tell me that you believe in all this crap? So, you followed me from the fucking Lounge?" Roy laughs, "Yeah, that's crazy ain't it." Roy pulls out the cloth. "Oh yeah, I found this on your table." John cringes, "I won't be needing that bro." Roy smiles and places it back into his robe, "I thought so." John and Roy stare at the murals. "I'll tell you something bro. my life was pretty fucked up until I met you." Roy sips the water. "Oh yeah?"

John continues, "Yeah, I thought I was crazy, until you came along. It dawns on me; I don't have anything on you. Your gone, but me. Hell, I'm sane." "I hope I never get as fucked up in the head as you bro." Roy grins, "Now that's on the real." John agrees, "Yeah, that's on the real." John stands; he feels a load off his chest. "I think I'm going to the pawn shop tomorrow, I could cash in on these babies." John pats the guns under his jacket. Roy smiles, "Yeah, that's cool man." John just stands, staring at the crucifix. Roy looks up, "You sure you don't want one of these waters?" John bust out laughing. It's the first time Roy's seen him smile. Without looking at Roy, John places his hand out, "Smack."

The bottle slaps in Johns hand. "It's been real cool bro; don't get bit by any bats tonight." "Yeah, you too." Roy watches, there's a spring in Johns step, his boots squeaks as he begins out the door and turns, "Oh yeah, what ever happened between you and that angel chick?" Roy smiles "Are you kidding me man, I made all that shit up just to fuck with you." John excites, "I figured that." He starts out, stops and turns, "Now that Missti chick, if I were you, I would have tagged that." Roy nods while John walks out, "Later bro!" Roy throws his hand up, "Yeah, later on!"

The door shuts; the Gargoyle takes another sip and smiles. There's nothing like the feeling one gets when they know that what they do is helpful, but even more so, that when they do something, that it's really them, just being themselves. Roy steps out of the church, the rain whistles in his ear, it almost sounds like the sweetness of nothings. Warmth overflows his mind, the rains not so cold inside. The wind rustles the street sign. When it rains, it pours; perhaps the sun will shine tomorrow.

Something's in the air, he can almost taste it. The silence hits his soul; a whisper echoes his heart. Roy turns; he feels it. "Bam!" He flies into the street, flipping onto his feet. The rain blinds his view. "Pow!" His jaw feels an awkward sharpness, and then goes numb." He stands; he didn't see that one coming. The pain in his jaw, no one's ever hit him so hard. "Ka-pow!" Roy lands in front of the coffee shop, breaking the metal chair in pieces. He springs to his feet. His eyes sharpen through the wet darkness. A Serge of energy overcomes him; he anticipates a strike and dodges. "Ka-boom!" Roy catches the soaring punch and pulls the assailant over him, kicking as he sends them sailing into the telephone pole; it splinters, sparks fizzle from the line. The creature pounces from the ground and lands in front of him, sending electrifying jabs. Roy matches the jabs and blocks each punch, but is only able to concentrate on the sending hands. "Who is this guy?"

Roy doesn't realize it, but he moves at speeds he's never tasted before. An eloping couple walks and stops under the coffee shop. They see lightning hit. They witness a light show that will be remembered to their grave. Roy feels the movement; he ducks and kicks, but is blocked. A kick goes for his underside, as he blocks, protecting his royals. "Boom!" Roy lands on his feet and looks up. His eyes grow big, he speaks, "Michael!" "Bam, Kaboom, Pow!" The couple watches the lightning arc the ground; Roy becomes a bolt of energy. The sky, lights up, the streetlights blow out. Lightning volts hit every wood and metal object within the city block.

A small cloud forms under their feet, Michael and Roy throw punches. "Sha-Bam!" Michael punches Roy's eye, sending him down to the ground; a lightning bolt hit's the ground, it's Roy. He stands, Michael charges, "Boom!" the glass in the department store shatters, Michael slides across, landing into the lingerie department, toppling clothes. She rebounds, not a word out of her mouth as she jolts at him. Michael dashes for him, "Foop!" She flies into the tree; it burst into flames. "Bam, Ka-Bam!" blows exchange, they both land punches to the face. Blood spurts out her mouth, but soon retracts, sealing her wound. She goes for his neck, but her hand's trap, as Roy sends her on her back. He mounts her, "Tall, fricken, Amazon bitch!"

Roy releases her hold as his right hand punches her mouth, sending blood across her mouth onto the pavement; the blood rolls like mercury and finds the opening, sealing her cut. She catches his second punch. As his arms push hers down, she lets out a gasp; Roy's strong. Straining, their arms shake as his strength overtakes hers. "Thump!" her hands hit's the ground above her head. Roy gets a close look at the angel. Her eyes are oval shaped, crystal blue; Roy feels her intelligence. Distracted by her eyes, she flips him over; her legs are much longer. "Bam, Bam, Bam!" Metallic blood flies from Roy's mouth, Bam, Bam, Bam! His eyes begin to roll. Michael is on top and lands punches left and right. "Flump, Pow, Thump!" Roy's hands grow limp. He manages to free his left hand, but it's not fast enough to stop her blows. "Boom, Bam, Pop!" For the first time, he feels pain and is out of breath. His hand attempts to scratch her face, but she smacks it away and rails on his face again, and again; Roy feels the knots, he's going to pass out. He gargles blood and hardly sees through his swollen eye. Spitting up blood, he speaks, "Okay, okay, you win, you win, I give up." His hand attempts to reach at her face to stop the blows. "Bam, Thump!" Roy reaches, only to touch the rain before him, he can't see. Each time he reaches up, she pushes his hands back. His voice goes weak, "Okay, I quit, I give up, you win." She holds his hands, the rain falls into his bloody eyes, the battle is over. His face feels like he hit a truck with it. She gazes, waiting. As she stares, she knows that it is only a matter of time before he heals. A soft voice whispers into his ears, "What do you see in a kiss?" The wetness is tasted, but it's not the rain, something's sweet, but it's not honey. He struggles to breathe, but gags for air. The warmth of lips presses against his; it takes his breath away. Roy's eyes begins to focus, the soft white face lifts away as she sits on his chest and stares, tilting her head as if to await his reaction. His eye begins to heal, the metallic blood repairs his wounds, Roy focuses, it's Michael.

The rain feels warm, the sky is silk, what is seen is the beauty of desire. A tug is felt, the sword slips from his waist, Michael receives her pride. A smile graces her eyes as she lifts herself up, her head looks towards the rain. "Ka-Pow!" the lightning flash; the moment is treasured for a lifetime. Roy stands; he wonders what the hell just happened. He looks up, nothing. He looks down, there, sets a white cloth, soaking in the rain. He picks up the cloth and opens it, revealing the Manna. His sore jaw bites into the softness, a smile zips across his face. What is seen in a kiss, is the desire of ones love; The Gargoyle knows who he is. Though the storm may come, there's always sunshine to follow; The Gargoyle sets for home.

The End

The dedication of this book is in honor of the persons who served our country to keep America free. To my Dad, Specialist-Four Roy C. Johnson, Retired Veteran 82nd Airborne Division, The United States Army, Navy, Marines, Air force, National Guard, Coast Guard, National Security Agency, Department of Defense, Central Intelligence Agency, Elite forces, and the Boy and Girl Scouts of America. Let Freedom reign!

website: www.bigjrecords.com email: johnsonsings@hotmail.com